"What has happened?" Zahir demanded urgently, straightening to his full six feet three inches of height, his lean, powerful body tensing like the army officer he had been into immediate battle readiness.

His face unusually flushed, his aide Akram came to an abrupt halt as he belatedly recalled the niceties of court etiquette. "My apologies for the interruption, your Majesty—"

"Akram…?" Zahir prompted impatiently. "I have a meeting in thirty minutes—"

"It's…*her!* That woman you married!" Akram recovered his tongue abruptly. "She's out there in the streets of our capital city shaming you even as we speak!"

Sapphire—the one mistake he had ever made and the payback had been unforgettably brutal. He had endured indescribable punishment to keep her as his wife for even a year. She owed him—she definitely owed him. She had used and abused him before walking away unharmed and incalculably richer. Maybe it was finally payback time, Zahir reflected grimly. And the very thought of Sapphire being in his power was the most seductive image that Zahir had indulged in for years.

A Bride for a BILLIONAIRE

The men who have everything finally meet their match!

The Marshall sisters have carved their own way in the world for as long as they can remember.
So if some arrogant billionaire thinks he can sweep in and whisk them off their stilettos,
he's got another think coming!

It will take more than a private jet and a wallet full of cash to win over these feisty, determined women. Luckily these men enjoy a challenge and have more than their bank accounts going for them!

You read Kat Marshall's story in

A RICH MAN'S WHIM

May 2013

This month, read Sapphire Marshall's story in

THE SHEIKH'S PRIZE

June 2013

Look out for more scandalous Marshall exploits coming soon!

Lynne Graham

THE SHEIKH'S PRIZE

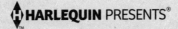

Recycling programs
for this product may
not exist in your area.

ISBN-13: 978-0-373-13151-8

THE SHEIKH'S PRIZE

Copyright © 2013 by Lynne Graham

All rights reserved. Except for use in any review, the reproduction or utilization of this work in whole or in part in any form by any electronic, mechanical or other means, now known or hereafter invented, including xerography, photocopying and recording, or in any information storage or retrieval system, is forbidden without the written permission of the publisher, Harlequin Enterprises Limited, 225 Duncan Mill Road, Don Mills, Ontario M3B 3K9, Canada.

This is a work of fiction. Names, characters, places and incidents are either the product of the author's imagination or are used fictitiously, and any resemblance to actual persons, living or dead, business establishments, events or locales is entirely coincidental.

This edition published by arrangement with Harlequin Books S.A.

For questions and comments about the quality of this book, please contact us at CustomerService@Harlequin.com.

® and TM are trademarks of Harlequin Enterprises Limited or its corporate affiliates. Trademarks indicated with ® are registered in the United States Patent and Trademark Office, the Canadian Trade Marks Office and in other countries.

Printed in U.S.A.

ll about the author…
ynne Graham

orn of Irish/Scottish parentage, **LYNNE GRAHAM** has lived in Northern Ireland all her life. She has one brother. She grew up in seaside village and now lives in a country house surrounded by a woodland garden, which is wonderfully private.

ynne first met her husband when she was fourteen; they married fter she completed a degree at Edinburgh University. Lynne wrote her first book at fifteen—it was rejected everywhere. She tarted writing again when she was at home with her first child. t took several attempts before she was published and she has never forgotten the delight of seeing that book for sale at the local newsagents.

Lynne always wanted a large family, and she now has five children. Her eldest, her only natural child, is in her twenties and is a university graduate. Her other children, who are every bit as dear to her heart, are adopted: two from Sri Lanka and two from Guatemala. In Lynne's home, there is a rich and diverse cultural mix, which adds a whole extra dimension of interest and discovery to family life.

The family has two pets. Thomas, a very large and affectionate black cat, bosses the dog and hunts rabbits. The dog is Daisy, an adorable but not very bright white West Highland terrier, who loves being chased by the cat. At night, the dog and cat sleep together in front of the kitchen stove.

Lynne loves gardening and cooking, collects everything from old toys to rock specimens, and is crazy about every aspect of Christmas.

CHAPTER ONE

ZAHIR RA'IF QUARISHI, hereditary king of the gulf state of Maraban, leapt up from behind his desk when his younger brother, Akram, literally burst into his office.

'What has happened?' Zahir demanded urgently, straightening to his full six feet three inches of height, his lean powerful body tensing like the army officer he had been into immediate battle readiness.

His face unusually flushed, Akram came to an abrupt halt to execute a jerky bow as he belatedly recalled the niceties of court etiquette.' My apologies for the interruption, Your Majesty—'

'I assume there's a good reason,' Zahir conceded, his rigidity easing as he read Akram's troubled expression and recognised that something of a more private and personal nature had precipitated his impulsive entry to one of the very few places in which Zahir could usually depend on receiving the peace he required to work.

Akram stiffened, embarrassment claiming his open good-natured face. 'I don't know how to tell you this—'

'Sit down and take a deep breath,' Zahir advised calmly, his innate natural assurance taking over as he settled his big frame down into an armchair in the corner of the room and rested his piercing dark-as-night eyes on the younger man while moving a graceful hand to urge him to sit down as well. 'There's nothing we can't discuss. I will never be as intimidating as our late father.'

At that reminder, Akram turned deadly pale, for their late and unlamented parent had been as much of a tyrant and a bully in the royal palace with his family as he was in his role as a ruler over what had once been one of the most backward countries in the Middle East. While Fareed the Magnificent, as he had insisted on being called, had been in power, Maraban's oil wealth had flowed only one way into the royal coffers while their people continued to live in the Dark Ages, denied education, modern technology and adequate medical support. It had been three years since Zahir took the throne and the changes he had immediately instigated still remained a massive undertaking. Angrily conscious that his brother worked just about every hour of the day in his determination to improve the lives of his subjects, Akram suddenly dreaded giving Zahir the news he had learned. Zahir never mentioned his first marriage. It was too controversial a topic, Akram acknowledged awkwardly. How could it not be? His brother had paid a high price for defying their late father and marrying a foreigner from a different culture. That he had done so for a woman clearly unworthy of his faith could only be an additional source of aggravation.

'Akram…?' Zahir prompted impatiently. 'I have a meeting in thirty minutes.'

'It's…*her!* That woman you married!' Akram recovered his tongue abruptly. 'She's out there in the streets of our capital city shaming you even as we speak!'

Zahir froze and frowned, his spectacular bone structure tightening beneath taut skin the colour of honey, his wide sensual mouth compressing hard. 'What the hell are you talking about?'

'Sapphire's here filming some television commercial for cosmetics!' Akram told him in fierce condemnation, resenting what he saw as an inexcusable insult to his elder brother.

Zahir's lean strong hands clenched into fists. 'Here?' he repeated in thunderous disbelief. 'Sapphire is filming *here* in Maraban?'

'Wakil told me,' his brother told him, referring to one of Zahir's former bodyguards. 'He couldn't believe his eyes when he recognised her! It's lucky that our father refused to announce your marriage to our people—I never thought we'd live to be grateful for that…'

Zahir was stunned at the idea that his ex-wife could have *dared* to set a single foot within the borders of his country. Rage and bitterness flamed through his taut powerful frame and he sprang restively upright again. He had tried not to be bitter, he had tried even harder to forget his failed marriage…only that was a little hard to do when your ex became an internationally famous supermodel, featuring in countless magazines and newspapers and even once in a giant advertising hoarding over Times Square. In truth a mere five years ago he had been a sitting duck of a target for a cunning schemer of Sapphire Marshall's ilk and that lowering awareness had left an indelible stain on his masculine ego. At twenty-five years of age he had, thanks to his father's oppression, still been a virgin, ignorant of the West and Western women, but although he hadn't had a clue he had at least *tried* to make his marriage work. His bride, on the other hand, had refused to make the smallest effort to sort out their problems. He had fought hard to keep a wife who didn't want to be his wife, indeed who couldn't even bear for him to touch her.

More fool him, he reflected with hard cynicism, for he was no longer an innocent when it came to women. The explanation for Sapphire's extraordinary behaviour had become clear as crystal to him once he shed his idealistic assumptions about his wife's honour: his bride had only married him because he was wealthy beyond avarice and a prince, *not* because she cared about him. Unpardonably, her goal in marrying him had simply been the rich pay-off that would follow their divorce. He had married a woman with all the heart of a cash register and she had, not only, ripped him off but also got away scot free while he had paid in spades. At that reflection, his even white teeth ground together, tiny gold flames igniting in his fierce eyes. If only he had been dealing with her in the present as a male who now knew the score, he would have known exactly how to handle her.

'I'm sorry, Zahir,' Akram muttered in the seething

silence, ill at ease with the rare dark fury that had flared in his brother's face. 'I thought you had a right to know that she'd had the cheek to come here.'

'It's five years since I divorced her,' Zahir pointed out harshly, his lean strong face impassive. 'Why should I care what she does?'

'Because she's an embarrassment!' Akram rushed to declare. 'Imagine how you would feel if the media found out that she was once your wife! She must be shameless and without conscience to come to Maraban to make her stupid commercial!'

'This is all very emotive stuff, Akram,' Zahir countered, reluctantly touched by his brother's concern on his behalf. 'I'm grateful you told me but what do you expect me to do?'

'Throw her and her film crew out of Maraban!' his brother told him instantly.

'You are still young and impetuous, my brother,' Zahir replied drily. 'The paparazzi follow my ex-wife everywhere she goes. Try to picture the likely consequences of deporting a world-famous celebrity. Why would I want to create headlines to alert the world's media to a past that is more wisely left buried?'

When Akram had finally departed, still incredulous that his brother had failed to express a desire for retribution, Zahir made several phone calls that would have astonished the younger man. It was a supreme irony but Zahir's coolly astute brain was perpetually at all-out war with the volatile passion of his temperament. While it made no logical sense whatsoever he wanted the chance to see Sapphire in the flesh again. Did that desire imply that he still had some lingering need for closure where she was concerned? Or was it simple and natural curiosity because he was currently facing the prospect of having to take another wife? Once, in a desperate search for a solution to his seemingly incurable problems with Sapphire, Zahir had read books about all sorts of strange subjects before he finally accepted that the simplest explanation of the apparently inexplicable was usually the closest to the truth. Since then events in his ex-wife's life had suggested that his sceptical convictions about her true character were spot-on. He had wed a gold-digging social climber with not an atom of true feeling for him. After all, he was well aware that Sapphire was now cosily ensconced in a live-in relationship with the award-winning Scottish wildlife photographer, Cameron McDonald. Presumably she wasn't having any difficulty bedding *him*… Zahir's dark eyes burned afresh like golden flames at that incendiary thought.

Saffy dutifully angled her hot face into the flow of air gushing from the wind machine so that her mane of blonde hair wafted back in a cloud over her shoulders. Not an atom of her growing irritation and discomfort showed on her flawless features. Saffy was never less than professional when she was working. But how many times had her make-up already needed retouched in the stifling heat? It was simply melting off her face. How many times had the set security had to interrupt filming to make the crowd of over-excited spectators back away to give her colleagues the space to work? Coming to Maraban to film the Desert Ice cosmetics commercial had been a foolish mistake. The support systems the film crew took for granted were non-existent.

'Give me *that* sexy look, Saffy...' Dylan, the photographer, urged pleadingly. 'What is wrong with you this week? You're not on form—'

And as if someone had zapped her with an electrified cattle prod, Saffy struggled to switch on the expression he wanted because she hated the fact that anyone should have noticed that anything was amiss with her mood. Inside her head, she fought to focus on the fantasy that never failed to ignite that much vaunted look of desire on her face. So ironic, she reflected momentarily, so very *cruelly* ironic that she should have to focus on what she had often dreamt of and never yet managed to experience in reality. But when she was working a shoot costing her clients thousands of pounds was not the time to allow all that old bad stuff to resurface. With the strong determination that was the backbone of her temperament, Saffy forced the distressing memories back down into her subconscious again and then mentally searched to extract the required familiar image: a man with jet-black hair down to his broad brown shoulders, a man who positively oozed raw animal magnetism from every pore with a lean powerfully naked body encased in warm gilded skin. In every image he would slowly turn his head to look at her, revealing fiercely stunning eyes of gold surrounded by black lashes so lush they acted like eye liner on a guy already so savagely masculine and passionate that at one glance he took her breath away. And all those wretched frustrating responses swam back through her taut body in a wave, her nipples beading below the scrap of silk she wore, her entire body dampening with shocking awareness.

'That's it...that's exactly it!' Dylan crooned in enthusiasm, leaping around her posed figure to take photos from different angles as she shifted position with languorous ease, that image inside her head like an indelible tattoo below her skin. 'Lower your lids a little more—we want to see that eye shadow...brilliant, sweetheart, now *pout* that gorgeous mouth...'

A couple of minutes passed before with a tiny jerk of displacement, Saffy returned to the present and was suddenly plunged back into the heat, the noise and the curious crowds, her huge bluer-than-blue eyes reflecting her discomfiture at the massive attention they were attracting. But Dylan had got the shots he wanted and he leapt around like a maniac punching the air with satisfaction. Her single-minded concentration on her role gone now, she looked out above the crowds and saw a vehicle parked at the height of a giant rolling ochre-coloured sand dune with a robed figure standing nearby holding something in his hand that glinted in the sun.

Zahir had his high-definition binoculars trained on his stunningly beautiful ex-wife. With her glorious mane of golden hair blowing back from her face like a sheet of gleaming silk and seated atop a pile of giant fake ice cubes, she would have looked spectacularly eye-catch-ing by any standards. But in the beauty stakes, Sapphire occupied a category all of her own and the sight of her took Zahir's hot-blooded temper to new and dangerous heights. He was outraged that she was appearing in public in Maraban clad in only a couple of scraps of azure silk that displayed the surprisingly bountiful mounds of her breasts, the smooth skin of her now bejewelled midriff and the incredible svelte stretch of her very long and perfect legs.

He watched the men involved in the shoot dart slavishly around Sapphire, offering her drinks and food and fussing with her hair and her face, and he wondered with vicious coarseness which of them had had the pleasure of her beautiful body. After all, she might live with Cameron McDonald, but the UK tabloids had, nonetheless, exposed the fact that she had had several affairs with other men. Clearly she was anything but a faithful lover. Of course, it was possible that Cameron and Sapphire enjoyed a civilly negotiated 'open' relationship, but Zahir was not impressed by that possibility or even by the concept of open relationships. He didn't sleep around, he had never slept around even when he finally had the freedom to make such choices. His ex-wife had to be a bit of a slut, he decided with dark brooding bitterness, his lean strong face set granite hard at the acknowledgement. He had married an embryo slut and, worst of all, she was a slut he *still* lusted after. At that final disturbing admission, Zahir ground his even white teeth while perspiration beaded his upper lip, his tall, powerful body furiously tense and aggressively aroused by his perusal of that perfect body and even more perfect face.

Sapphire, the one mistake he had ever made and the payback had been unforgettably brutal. He had endured indescribable punishment to keep her as his wife for even a year. She owed him, she definitely *owed* him for twelve months of unadulterated hell. Add in the millions she had received from him since the charade of their marriage finally ran aground in a divorce and he had every right to feel ill-done by, every right to still be aggrieved and hostile. She had used and abused him before walking away unharmed and considerably richer. Maybe it was finally payback time, Zahir reflected grimly, his adrenalin spiking at the idea. And bearing in mind that she and her film crew had chosen to come to Maraban and film without the permission of the relevant authority, she had put herself and her precious high-flying career in his power. And the very thought of Sapphire being in his power was the most seductive image that Zahir had indulged in for years. He lowered the binoculars, thinking fast, squashing the disconcerting logical objections already trying to assail him to persuade him to restrain his primal responses. It wouldn't be the same between them now, he reasoned angrily; he was not the same man. This time around he had the weapons to *make* her want him back.

That process of self-persuasion was incredibly seductive. Throughout his life Zahir had very rarely done what *he* wanted to do, for the necessity of always considering the needs of others had taken precedence. But why shouldn't he put his own desires first for once? He had already checked Sapphire's schedule and she was due to leave Maraban within hours, an awareness that merely made him all the more single-minded. Zahir made his plans there and then with ruthless cool and the same kind of fierce, almost suicidal resolution that had once persuaded him to take a foreign wife without first asking his despotic father's permission. As that reality and comparison briefly occurred to him he stubbornly suppressed the piercing shard of unease it awakened.

With a sense of merciful release from the strain of being on show, Saffy stepped into the site trailer to change. She shed the skimpy silk bandeau and slashed skirt and peeled off the fake navel jewel before donning white linen trousers and an aqua tee. In a couple of hours she would be on her way home and saying goodbye to the joys of Maraban couldn't come quickly enough as far as she was concerned. After all, it was the last place in the world she would have chosen to visit, but civil unrest in a neighbouring country had led to a last-minute change of location and nobody had been willing to listen to her necessarily vague objections. But then the fact that nobody had a clue about her past connection to Maraban or Zahir was a relief. Thankfully that period of her life before fame had claimed her remained a deep dark secret.

So, in spite of all he had once had to say on the score of corrupt hereditary rulerships, Zahir had still ended up taking the throne to become a king. But then, according to what she had read in the newspapers, the citizens of Maraban had not had a clue what to do with the offer of democracy and had instead rallied round their popular hero prince, who had rebelled with the army against his old horror of a father to protect the people. There were pictures of Zahir everywhere: she had noticed one in the hotel foyer with a vase of flowers set beneath it rather like a little sacred shrine. Her lush mouth twisted as she questioned the thread of bitterness powering her thoughts. He was honourable, a big fan of justice and was very probably an excellent king, she conceded grudgingly. It really wasn't fair to resent him for what he couldn't have helped. Their marriage had been a disaster and even now her thoughts slid away from the memories with alacrity. He had broken her heart and dumped her when she failed to deliver and she wasn't really sure that it was fair to hate him for that when by that stage she had been urging him to divorce her for months. Everyone made choices, everyone had to live with those choices and a happy ending wasn't always included.

But she had a good life, she reminded herself doggedly as the security team cleared a path for her through the crush of spectators to the waiting limo that would whisk her back to the airport. She now had three glorious days of freedom to look forward to, and a tired sigh escaped her as she touched an admiring fingertip to the silky petal of an impossibly perfect blossom in the beautiful bouquet displayed in a vase inside the limo, while only vaguely wondering where the flowers had come from. When she got back to London, she would first catch up with her sisters, one who was pregnant, one who was desperate to conceive and one who was still at school. Her eldest sister, Kat, was thirty-six and considering fertility treatment while still being full of the newly married joys of her life with her Russian billionaire. After a sticky interview with her tough brother-in-law, Mikhail Saffy was a little less enamoured of her sibling's blunt-spoken husband. Mikhail had demanded to know why Saffy hadn't offered to help Kat when her sister had run into serious debt. Well, *hello,* Saffy thought back angrily—Kat had never told Saffy that she was in trouble and, even if she had, Saffy knew she would have found it a challenge to come up with that kind of cash at short notice. Having made a major commitment early in her career to help support an African school for AIDS orphans, Saffy lived comfortably but not in luxury.

Saffy's twin, Emmie, was pregnant and Saffy had not been surprised to learn that Emmie didn't have a supportive man by her side. Saffy was painfully aware that her twin did not forgive those who hurt or offended her and in all probability the father of Emmie's child had made that mistake. Saffy knew better than anyone how inflexible her sibling could be because the relationship between the twins had long been tense and troubled. Indeed Saffy could never suppress the surge of the guilt that attacked her whenever she saw her sister. As young children she and Emmie had been very close but events during their troubled teen years had ripped them apart and the two young women had never managed to repair that breach. Saffy would never forget the injuries that *her* reckless behaviour had inflicted on her twin sister or the many years of suffering that Emmie had endured as a result. Some things were just too bad to be forgiven, Saffy acknowledged sadly.

In any case, Mikhail and Kat would undoubtedly assist Emmie in her struggles as a single mum—certainly, Saffy knew better than to offer assistance that would be richly resented. But she could not understand why Emmie had chosen to make a big secret of her baby's paternity. Saffy winced at that thought. While it was true that Saffy had never told her sisters the humiliating truth about her own failed marriage, she felt that she had had good reasons for her silence, not the least of which was the embarrassing fact that she had totally ignored Kat's plea that Saffy get to know Zahir better and for longer *before* she married him. Just common sense really, Saffy conceded wryly. Getting married at eighteen to a guy you had only known a couple of months and had never lived with had been an act of insanity. As immature and idealistic as most teenagers with little experience of independent life, Saffy had struggled from the outset with the role of being a wife in a different culture. And while she had struggled, Zahir had steadily grown more and more distant, not to mention his penchant for disappearing for weeks at a time on army manoeuvres just when she needed him most. Yes, she had made mistakes…but then *so had he*.

Satisfied with that appraisal, which approportioned

equal blame for what had gone wrong in the past, Saffy emerged from her reverie and noticed in surprise that the limo was travelling down a wide empty road that strongly reminded her of an airport runway. As the route back to the airport entailed travelling through Maraban city, she frowned, gazing out in confusion at the emptiness of the desert surrounding her on all sides. Strewn with stones and occasional large volcanic rock formations, the bleak desert terrain was interrupted by little vegetation. And so pervasive was the march of the sand that it was steadily encroaching on the road, blurring its outlines.

Saffy had never warmed to Zahir's natural preference for a lot of sand in his vicinity, had never learned to adjust to the extremes of heat or to admire the austerity of such a landscape. Where on earth were they going? Could the driver be taking another route to avoid the city traffic, such as it was? Her smooth brow creasing, she leant forward to rap the glass partition to attract the driver's attention, but although she saw his eyes flicker in the rear-view mirror to glance in her direction he made no attempt to respond to her. While Saffy was annoyed at being ignored, his behaviour also awakened the first stirrings of genuine apprehension and Saffy rapped the glass harder and shouted for him to stop. What on earth was the stupid man playing at? She didn't want to miss her flight home and she didn't have time to waste.

As she withdrew her fingers from the glass her knuckle brushed against the flowers in the vase and for the first time she noticed the envelope attached to them. She snatched it up and ripped it open to extract a typed card.

It is with great pleasure that I invite you to enjoy my hospitality for the weekend.

What on earth? Saffy stared down at the unsigned card. Who was inviting her where and why? Was this why her uncommunicative driver was travelling in the wrong direction? Her even white teeth gritted in angry frustration. Had her lightly clad appearance at the shoot caught the eye of some local randy sheikh? Possibly even the guy in the sand dunes with the binoculars? What did he think she was? Dial-a-tart? No, no, *no!* Her blue eyes flashed like twin blue fires. No way was she sacrificing her one free weekend to pandering to the ego of yet another rich man, keen to assume that the very fact she made her living by her face and body meant that she was an easy lay available to the highest bidder! Desert Ice cosmetics was always willing to serve her up to VIPs as the face of its product and the somewhat racy reputation bestowed on her by the tabloids encouraged the wrong expectations and made rejecting amorous men even more of a challenge.

No way on earth was she spending her weekend with some man she hadn't even met! She dug through her bag in search of her cell phone, intending to ring one of her colleagues for assistance, but she couldn't find her phone and only finally accepted that it wasn't there after she had tipped out the contents of her bag on the seat beside her. She had had her phone in her hand before she got changed, she recalled with a frown. She had set it down…and clearly she hadn't picked it up again! She ground her teeth together and just for the sake of it attempted to open the door beside her. She wasn't surprised to find it locked and it really didn't matter, she conceded ruefully, for she had no intention of risking serious injury by throwing herself out of a moving car.

Conscious of the anxious glances the driver was now giving her in the mirror, she lifted her head high, her brain working double time. She might feel as if she were being kidnapped, but that was a most unlikely interpretation of her situation in a country as old-fashioned and law-abiding as Maraban. In addition, no Arab host would want an unwilling guest in his home. Indeed making a guest uncomfortable was a big no-no in Marabani culture, so once she politely explained that she had a prior engagement and apologised for being unavailable, she would be free to leave again…only by that time she might well have missed her flight home. Her lush mouth took on a downward curve.

Only minutes later, the limo came to a halt by the side of the road and with a click the door beside her opened. Saffy's brow pleated as she climbed out and she thought about making a run for it. But a run for it to where? It was the hottest part of the day and she would burn to a crisp. In addition the road was still empty and they had travelled miles through unbroken desert. As she pondered the unavoidable fact that there was nowhere safe to run to, a large four-wheel-drive vehicle drew up at the other side of the road. The driver jumped out and

opened the passenger door wide while regarding her expectantly. Clearly it was an arranged meeting for her to
be transferred to another vehicle. Did she accept that?
Or fight it…but fight it with what? She glanced back
into the limo and studied the glass vase that held the
flowers. It was the work of a moment to smash the vase
against the built-in bar and retrieve a jagged piece of
glass, which she cupped awkwardly in her hand because
she didn't want to tighten her fingers and cut herself
on it. Straightening her slim shoulders, she crossed the
road and climbed into the four-wheel-drive. The door
slammed instantly behind her.

Was she in any true danger, she asked herself irrita-
bly, or was she at even greater risk of being swept along
by an over-confident belief that somehow she was still in
control of events? As soon as they arrived at their destination she would make it very clear that she wished to
return to the airport immediately and if anyone dared
to lay a single finger on her she would slash that person
with the glass. Now was not the time to wish she had
taken self-defence classes.

The vehicle moved off and performed a U-turn to
pass directly in front of the limo and drive down a stony
track that ran straight out into the desert. That change
in direction took Saffy very much by surprise and she
looked out of the windows in dismay at the giant loom-
ing sand dunes coming closer to tower all around them
as the rough track streaked doggedly ahead. It was very
bumpy and very hot because there seemed to be no air-
conditioning in the car. Perspiration beading her brow,

Saffy gripped the safety rail above her head and gritted her teeth, thinking that possibly she should have made a run for it while they were still on the highway. As the track inevitably vanished beneath the sand the powerful vehicle roared endlessly over the shallow mounds that had taken its place, forging a zigzagging path between the dunes. Finally, when every bone in her body felt as if it were rattling inside her skin, the vehicle began to climb up the steep side of a dune, the engine whining at the strain. At the top she peered out of the window and focused on the sole sign of civilisation within view: a stone fortress with tall walls and turrets that looked remarkably like an ancient crusader castle.

Oh, dear, she thought with a sinking heart, for it didn't look as though it would offer the comforts of a five-star hotel and where else could they possibly be heading? And who in their right mind would invite her to such a remote place? Aside of a herd of goats there was nothing moving in the castle's vicinity.

The car thundered down the slope towards the building and big black gates spread slowly open as they approached. Through the gates she glimpsed surprisingly lush greenery, a welcome sight to eyes strained by sand overload. The vehicle lurched to a halt and she breathed in slow and deep when she saw staff clustered round an arched entrance. Maybe it *was* a hotel; certainly it looked at least the equal of the one she had stayed at in the city. As Saffy stepped out heads bowed low and nobody looked directly at her and nobody spoke. Saffy was in no mood to speak anyway and she followed in the steps of the older man who shifted his hand to gain her attention. Her shoes clicked on a polished marble floor and the blessed coolness of air-conditioning chilled her hot damp skin but nothing could have prepared her for the awe-inspiring sight that met her eyes. The amazingly spectacular hall stretched into seeming infinity in front of her. Fashioned of gleaming white marble and studded with gilded pillars and ornate mirrors, it was as unexpected in its sheer opulence inside those ancient walls as snow in the desert. She blinked in bewilderment, gazing up to scan the heavily decorated ceiling far above, which rejoiced in a gloriously well executed mural of a sunny blue sky dotted with exotic flying birds. A few feet ahead her guide hovered to wait for her to move on again.

Her mouth tightening, Saffy walked on to descend a shallow flight of stone stairs and walk through tall gilded doors into a vast sunlit room, which, although draped in luxury fabrics, was traditionally furnished in Eastern style with low divans and beautiful rugs carefully arranged around a central fire pit where coffee could be made and served in the same way as it might have been in a tent. It was a statement that her prospective host respected the old ways from the far-off years when the Marabani had been nomadic tribesmen. She pushed the piece of glass into her bag.

'Qu'est-ce que vous desirez, madame?'

Startled, Saffy turned her head to see a youthful maid eager to do her bidding, and well did she recall that sinking sensation at the familiar sound of the French language, which was more commonly spoken in Maraban than English. For a girl who had dismally failed her GCSE French exam, communicating in French had been a major challenge five years earlier.

'*Apportez des refraîchissements*...bring refreshments,' another voice interposed in fluent accented French as smooth as honey warmed by the sun. 'And in future use English to speak to Miss Marshall,' he advised.

Tiny hairs prickling eerily at the base of her skull, her eyes huge and her slim body trembling, Saffy stared in disbelief at the man in the doorway. In the corner of her eye the maid bent her head, muttered something that sounded terribly servile and backed swiftly out of the room through another exit.

'*Zahir...?*' Saffy framed in shaken disbelief.

CHAPTER TWO

'Who else?' Zahir enquired silkily as she backed away small step by small step.

Saffy's heart was in her mouth and she was desperately short of breath because her every instinct for self-preservation was pumping full-blown panic through her tall, slender length. Zahir? Zahir, the King of Maraban. *He* was responsible for bringing her to the castle/fortress/palace, whatever it was? *He* was the host who wanted her to enjoy his hospitality for the weekend? What kind of sense did that make for a male who had divorced her five years ago and never once since alluded to their former relationship in public?

Yet he stood there, effortlessly self-assured in a black cotton shirt and jeans, a casual outfit that however emanated designer chic, for both garments fitted his very tall, well-built frame to perfection. He was one of the very few men Saffy had to look up to even in heels because he was several inches over six feet. Unhappily the sheer impact of his unexpected appearance shattered her renowned composure. For so long she had told herself that memory must have lied, that if she were to meet him again she would not be so impressed as she had been at the tender age of eighteen. And yet there he stood, defying her every ego-boosting excuse. Luxuriant hair with the blue-black shine of polished jet accentuated his absolutely gorgeous face, drawing her attention to the slash of his high exotic cheekbones, the proud arch of his nose, the stubborn jut of his strong jawline and the beautifully defined, wide, sensual fullness of his mouth. He had the lean powerfully athletic physique of a Greek god. And the fiercely stunning dark eyes of a jungle predator. He wasn't safe; she saw that now. Zahir was not a man who played safe or who gave his woman the freedom to do her own thing, not when he had come to earth convinced of the fact that he always knew best. She had been way too innocent at eighteen and yet already damaged, she conceded painfully, much more damaged than either of them could ever have guessed. In spite of the surge of disturbing memories, butterflies still leapt and fluttered in her tummy at the stirring sight of him: dear heaven, she acknowledged in even greater shock, he could *still* rock her world.

In defiance of that disturbing conviction, Saffy flung her head high, shining layers of wheaten blonde hair sliding like heavy silk back from her face and tumbling off her shoulders. '*You're* responsible for bringing me here?' she demanded shakily, her voice embarrassingly breathy and insubstantial from the level of incredulity still gripping her. 'Why on earth would you do that?'

Eyes of heavenly blue clung to Zahir's lean dark face. His astute dark eyes narrowed, hardened, kindled to burning gold as he allowed himself a slow steady appraisal of her lithe figure. Tall and slim she might be, but unlike many models Sapphire had womanly curves and the fine cotton T-shirt she wore could not hide the high pouting curve of her breasts or their beaded tips, any more than her white linen trousers concealed the long supple line of her thighs, the delicious peachy swell of highly feminine hips below her tiny waist or the dainty elegance of her narrow ankles. The pulse at his groin kicked up hell in response and he clenched his teeth together, willing down that threat to his self-possession. If he was honest he had expected to be a little disappointed with her when he saw her again face to face, but if he was equally honest she was even more staggeringly lovely now than she had been as a teenager. Shorn of a slight hint of adolescent chubbiness, her flawless bone structure had fined down.

Zahir surveyed her with smoulderingly bright eyes, instantly resenting her effect on him. 'Since we parted, you've cost me over five million pounds. Maybe I was curious to see what I was paying for. Maybe I even thought I might be due something in return…'

Angry resentment surged from the base of Saffy's insecurity and discomfiture. How dared he talk back to her as if he had done nothing wrong?

'Just you stop right there… Are you out of your mind?' she blazed back at him full tilt. 'What the heck gives you the right to bring me here when I don't want to be here?'

'I wanted to speak to you.'

'But we've got nothing to talk about!' Saffy scissored back without pausing to draw breathe. 'I never expected to see you again in this lifetime and I don't want to speak to you, not even to find out why you're talking about five million pounds that I certainly didn't receive!'

'You're a liar,' he retorted quietly, using that deadly quietness he had always had the power to deploy once he had got her to screaming point. It was impossible to deflect Zahir from his target.

'I have to ask—on the score of the five million pounds you mentioned—what planet are you living on? I haven't had a penny from you since I started working!' Saffy snapped out of all patience while desperately trying to recapture her cool and with it her wits.

'Denial won't cut it,' Zahir scissored back with cool contempt. 'I have paid you substantial alimony since the day you left Maraban—'

'No way!' Saffy sizzled back at him, enraged by his condemnation. After all, she was very proud of her independence and of the fact that she had never taken advantage of his great wealth, believing as she had that their short-lived and unsuccessful marriage gave her no right to expect his continuing support. 'That is a complete lie, Zahir. You gave me money when I first left and I needed to use that until I started earning. But I never wanted alimony from you…I told my solicitor that and he must have informed you.'

'No, since your departure the money has been paid every month into a trust fund and none of it has ever been returned,' Zahir informed her with infuriating certainty. 'But at this moment I should warn you that that may not be your most pressing problem.'

Saffy gritted her teeth. She was shaking with rage and shocked by the speed with which her usually easy temper had gone skyward. She had forgotten, oh, dear heaven, she had actually forgotten how easily Zahir could push her buttons. 'Why? What may be my most pressing problem?' she slung back scornfully, hot pink adorning both her cheeks.

'You and your colleagues shot your commercial without first lodging a request for permission to do so from the Ministry of the Interior.'

'I know nothing about that!' Saffy proclaimed in instant dismissal of the charge. 'I've got nothing to do with the legal requirements or arrangements for filming abroad—I'm just the model. I go where I'm told and you had better believe that Maraban was the last place on earth I wanted to come!'

Zahir tensed, an even brighter sliver of gold lightening his dark eyes. 'Why so? Maraban is a beautiful country.'

'Surely that view depends on your standards of beauty?' Saffy snapped back with lashings of scorn. 'Maraban is eighty per cent desert!'

The gold effect in his eyes heightened to flame level. 'Had you still been my wife I would have been ashamed of your narrow outlook!'

Saffy loosed a cutting laugh. 'Mercifully for me I'm no longer your wife!'

The insult made him tense even more, his big shoulders squaring, the wall of his strong abdominal muscles tightening visibly below his shirt. His eyes held her fast, held her as completely as if he had her pinioned to a wall, those extraordinarily beautiful eyes of his set below well-defined ebony brows, eyes rimmed with thick curling black lashes and stormily bright with aggression. 'Mercifully for us both,' he murmured levelly.

Inexplicably his agreement wounded her and she sucked in a sudden surge of air to fill her deflated lungs in the seething silence and decided to concentrate on basics. 'So the shoot took place without permission from some authority—what does that mean?'

'That the film was confiscated at the hotel where you and the crew were staying,' Zahir advanced grimly.

Saffy took a hasty step forward. '*Confiscated?*' she repeated in horror. 'You can't do that!'

'I can do anything I like when people break the law in Maraban,' Zahir responded levelly. 'Filming was not authorised.'

'But you have the power to overlook it. I'm sure the company just made a mistake if they didn't seek permission. The location was changed at the very last minute—there probably wasn't time!' she protested. 'Is that why you've brought me here? To tell me this?'

'No…I wanted to see you again,' Zahir confided with shocking cool.

And she remembered the shock of that honest streak of his, his ability to cut through all the rubbish people could spout and hit the bottom line without hesitation or embarrassment. 'Why would you want to see me again?' she prompted stiltedly.

'You only have to look in the mirror to know why,' he fielded without skipping a beat. 'I want you. Just once I want what should have been mine when I married you and what you have since given to other men...'

Shock engulfed Saffy in a tidal wave. She moved back from him again in dismay, disbelief and bewilderment. Her ex wanted her to have sex with him?

'Unless, of course,' Zahir murmured silkily, 'you truly *do* find me physically repulsive...'

Saffy backed away another step, thinking that there was surely not a woman alive who could find Zahir repulsive. She certainly didn't; never had, in fact. Was that the impression she had left him with? Guilt rippled through her, for she was agonisingly aware that he could not possibly have overcome her problems for her five years earlier. It had taken years of therapy for Saffy to find the solution and to come to terms with what she had learned about herself during the process.

'If you can convince me that you do, I will let you go,' Zahir purred, literally stalking her across the room with fluid steps.

Zahir wanted to sleep with her. So, tell me something new, a wry little voice said inside her head. It was like being plunged back into her marriage without warning, unable to give him what he wanted and needed. The most appalling sense of inadequacy gripped her afresh. She had failed him and not surprisingly he was bitter. But that was no excuse whatsoever for his current behaviour. 'You virtually kidnapped me!' she accused rawly.

'I sent you flowers and an air-conditioned limo. How many kidnappers do that?'

'You've got to be crazy... I mean, are you even thinking about what you're doing?' Saffy gasped, stepping back against a piece of furniture and sidling sideways to avoid it and to keep moving further out of his reach.

'I don't *think* around you,' Zahir muttered flatly. 'I never did.'

Saffy was more than willing to kick his brain back into gear. 'Zahir, you're a king...royalty doesn't do stuff like this!'

Zahir flung back his darkly handsome head and laughed with rich appreciation, even white teeth flashing against his bronzed skin. 'Sapphire...my father kept a harem of a hundred concubines in this palace. Until very recently indeed, royalty did indeed do things that were neither socially nor morally acceptable.'

'Your father? Had a *harem* here?' Saffy parroted in consternation, her heart beating so fast as he stalked closer that she was convinced it might burst right out of her chest. She refused even to think of that nasty old man, Fareed, having had a hundred unfortunate women locked up to fulfil his gruesome requirements. It wasn't a surprise though: her father-in-law had been an out-and-out lech.

'I have no harem...no wife,' Zahir pointed out.

'Those are the only positives you have to offer in your own favour?' Her voice was careening up and down as if she were on a vocal seesaw. She was locked into his eyes, those amazingly beautiful amber eyes, which had struck her like a thunderbolt at eighteen across a crowded department store. 'Stay back...'

'No, been there, done that, paid the price,' Zahir countered, running a forefinger slowly down over her cheekbone so that in some strange way it seemed perfectly normal to turn her cheek into his hand.

Saffy looked up, clashed with his eyes, experienced a light-headed sensation that did nothing to collect her wits, and swallowed painfully. How could he be so gorgeous that she couldn't breathe? Why was it as if the world had stopped turning and had flung her off into space? She was completely disorientated by his proximity, the very heat she could feel filtering from his lean powerful body towards hers even though their only connection was the hand resting against her face. 'Zahir?'

He lowered his proud dark head. He's going to kiss me, he's going to kiss me, a crazily excited voice chanted inside her head and both anticipation and denial warred inside her. And then he *did,* firm, sensual lips circling hers, the pressure steadily deepening even as a shriek alarm of shock shrilled through her trembling body. He parted her lips, let his tongue dart between and it felt like the most erotic caress she had ever experienced because the taste and the flicker of movement inside her mouth were indescribably sexy. Heat burned in her pelvis, her nipples swelling taut, abrading the cotton covering them. That intoxicating intense physical reaction was exactly what she had wanted to feel for a long time but he was the very last man on earth she wanted to feel it with.

And yet she couldn't will herself to break free while his tongue tangled with hers, touching, tasting, *savouring,* a low growl breaking from his throat while his fingertips stroked her neck where it met her shoulder. Unholy pleasure was ricocheting through her treacherous body as it awakened to sudden life, hot, damp sensation tingling at her feminine core while her breasts swelled and ached. Gathering every atom of her strength, she pushed her hand forcefully against a wide muscular shoulder and broke free. 'No…no, I don't want this!'

His gaze filled with sardonic amusement, Zahir studied her hectically flushed face with satisfaction. 'Liar,' he said thickly. 'You always liked my mouth on you.'

Saffy felt the rush of heat below her skin and momentarily closed her eyes while she blocked him out and fought for recovery. He was a demon kisser. That far, *they* had worked and the chemistry had misleadingly suggested a match made in heaven. In that instant, she loathed him for bringing the past alive again and reminding her of exactly what she yearned to find in another man's arms. Frustration filled her. Been there, done that, as he had said, although they hadn't actually *done it.* Did he feel cheated? Was that why he had brought her here? Why did he think that anything would have changed between them? It was not as if he knew what she had gone through in search of a cure. Crushing out that torrent of curious questions and musings, Saffy concentrated on the here and now.

'I want transport to the airport and the film that was confiscated,' she told him drily, straightening her slender shoulders to stand up to him.

Zahir viewed her from beneath the cloak of his lush black lashes, dark eyes bright as stars. 'It's not happening.'

'Then what would it take to make it happen?' Saffy prompted, determined to sort the situation out by taking the practical approach that generally served her well in difficult situations. 'That missing money you mentioned? I promise I'll look into that mystery and sort it out as soon as I get back to London.'

'Don't try to avoid the real issue here—I want *you...*'

Her mouth ran dry and her skin ran hotter than hot as he lounged back against the wall beside him and she noticed, really couldn't help noticing by the close fit of his jeans that he was aroused. She turned her head away, her tummy flipping even as she recognised the healthy discovery that the awareness of his arousal no longer made her feel threatened. 'But we can't always have what we want,' she pointed out tautly, hanging onto her cool with difficulty. 'And you know that bringing me here is crazy. Your people would be scandalised by this set-up.'

'I'm a single man and not a eunuch.'

'You're also intelligent and fair—at least you used to be,' Saffy countered with determination.

'Then you will understand that I seek justice.'

'Because you didn't get either the wedding night or the bride of your dreams you think you can magically turn the clock back?' Saffy lifted a fair brow. 'Good luck with that without a time machine.'

'You're *staying*,' Zahir declared with razor-sharp emphasis. 'And I don't want the girl you were five years ago. I want the woman you are now.'

'But the woman I am now is living with another man,' Saffy slotted in curtly, shooting the last bolt in her rejection routine, which she usually regarded as worth using only at the last ditch but his sheer persistence was ruffling more than her feathers

'And he shares you with whomever you choose to stray with,' Zahir retorted, unimpressed, his wide sensual mouth compressing with speaking derision.

Saffy stiffened as though he had slapped her in the face. Evidently he had come across the silly stories about her that the tabloids printed and believed them, actually believed that she slept around whenever she felt like it. But then she had only to be pictured emerging from a man's apartment for the press to assume she was engaged in an affair, but the truth was that she had some very good male friends, whom she visited, and had learned to treat the reports with amusement, for there was really nothing she could do to stop lies about her appearing in print. That, she had learnt, was the price of a life lived in the public eye.

'That is not true. Cameron and I are very close. He's my best friend,' Saffy admitted, throwing her head high, reluctant to lie to him about that relationship but happy to take advantage of his ignorance if it acted as another barrier between them.

'I don't want to be your best friend. I want to be your lover.'

Saffy's lovely face snapped tight and turned pale. 'And we both know how that panned out five years ago,' she reminded him flatly. 'Let me go, Zahir. Bringing me here is reckless and illogical.'

Zahir studied her with veiled eyes, a grimly amused smile tugging at the corners of his handsome male mouth. 'Perhaps that's why it feels so good.'

Saffy had shot her last reasonable bolt and she was stunned by his indifference. 'You don't know what you're saying.'

'I have never been so sure of anything,' he shot back in rebuttal.

The last string of restraint broke free inside Saffy. She had had a very long, hot and tiring day and now Zahir was plunging her into the nightmare of her better forgotten past. 'But you can't be serious…you can't *really* intend to keep me here against my will!'

'I will do nothing that causes you harm,' Zahir replied stubbornly.

'But keeping me here against my will is causing me harm! What gives you the idea that you can do this to me?' Saffy lashed back at him, her temper finally slipping its leash and her voice rising on a shrill note.

'The knowledge that I have achieved it. Your colleagues have been informed that you have accepted a private invitation to spend another few days in Maraban. Nobody will be looking for you or concerned that anything is amiss,' Zahir asserted with satisfaction.

'You *can't* do this to me!' Saffy erupted, infuriated by his self-assurance, his evident belief that he had covered all bases. 'And why? Nothing's going to happen between us. You're wasting your time!'

'No man looking at you could possibly believe that I was wasting my time in at least trying,' Zahir drawled with husky appreciation, his golden eyes resting on her delicate profile with possessive heat. 'It is a risk I take with pleasure.'

'But I *don't!*' Saffy slammed back at him in furious rebuttal. 'I didn't agree to this. Nobody tells me what to do or makes me stay somewhere I don't want to be and nothing on this earth is capable of persuading me to get into bed with you again, so you can forget that idea right now!'

'I will call Fadith to take you to your room…' Zahir pressed a button on the wall with a graceful brown hand, his bold profile set in uncompromising lines.

In outrage that he wasn't even taking heed of her objections, Saffy swept up a china vase on a stand and pitched it at him. It fell short and smashed against the edge of the fire pit to break into a hundred pieces.

Zahir enraged her by turning his handsome dark head and treating her to a slashing smile of very masculine amusement. 'Ah, that takes me back years. I had forgotten how you liked to throw things at me when you lost control of your temper. I will see you later when it is time to dine.'

And with that very cool and unruffled assurance, Zahir strolled out of the room and left her standing there in a tempestuous rage that she could do nothing more to vent with her target gone. Trembling from the force of her pent-up feelings, Saffy breathed in deep to find inner calm. He would pay; she would *make* him pay for this in spades!

CHAPTER THREE

FADITH REAPPEARED AND led the way down a corridor and up a flight of pale marble stairs. Shown into a room as traditionally furnished and comfortable as the room she had seen downstairs, Saffy breathed in deep. The furniture was ebony inlaid with gleaming mother-of-pearl and the bed was a fantasy four-poster hung in swirling silk that piled opulently on the floor at each corner. Saffy wandered into a bathroom with a sunken marble tub and every possible extra and suppressed a groan. As she returned to the bedroom Fadith was removing a tray from another maid's grasp to set it on a table.

'Thanks,' Saffy murmured, reluctantly lifting the mint drink she recalled from the year she had spent in Maraban. Maraban, the land that time forgot, she reflected grimly. She asked if there was any water and was shown a concealed refrigerator in a cupboard. She pulled out a chilled bottle and unscrewed the cap.

'Would you like a bath?' Fadith asked her then, clearly eager to be of service.

Saffy screened her mouth and faked a yawn before telling an outright lie to get rid of the younger woman.

'Perhaps later. I think I'll lie down and sleep for a while. It's very warm.'

Fadith pulled the blinds and scurried over to the bed to turn it down in readiness before departing. Playing safe, Saffy waited for a couple of minutes before heading off to explore. She had no intention of staying with Zahir and since there was no prospect of her being rescued she had to rescue herself. She walked across the vast landing on quiet feet, passing innumerable closed doors and peering out of windows into inner courtyards before finally heading downstairs. Ignoring the ground floor, she went down another flight into the basement, which she could see by the trolleys of cleaning equipment was clearly the servants' area. It was easy to identify the kitchens from the clatter of dishes and the buzz of voices and she gave it a wide berth. She stared out through a temptingly open rear door at the line of dusty vehicles parked outside while wondering what the chances were of any of them having keys left inside them. She wasn't stupid enough to think that she could walk out of the desert: she needed wheels to get back to the city. Without further hesitation she sped out into the heat and the first thing she saw was a four-wheel-drive full of soldiers at the far side of the courtyard. In dismay she dropped down into a crouch to hide behind a car. Of course there would be soldiers around to guard Zahir while he was in residence, she conceded ruefully. She inched up her head to peer into the car and then twisted to study its neighbour: there was no sign of keys left carelessly in the ignition. Meanwhile the soldiers trooped indoors. Saffy continued her seemingly fruitless search for a car to steal and dived behind a vehicle to avoid being seen when a couple of kitchen staff strolled out of the palace talking loudly.

One of them wished the other a good journey home in Arabic and she recognised the phrase as the young man threw his bag into the pickup and jumped into the driver's seat. He was going home? There was a good chance that he would be driving into the city. For a split second Saffy hesitated while she considered her options. The gates were guarded. It would be impossible for her to drive through them without being detected. Possibly stowing away in a vehicle being driven by a member of staff would be a cleverer move. Before she could lose her nerve, she scrambled over the tailgate and dived below the tarpaulin cover.

But the pickup didn't immediately move off as she had expected. In fact someone shouted to the driver and he got back out of the vehicle. She lay still, stiff with tension, listening to voices talking too fast for her to follow before the steps moved slowly away and she heard the driver moving back. Finally the door slammed again, the engine ignited and she expelled her breath in relief. Her original drive from the road down the track to the palace had been long and rough and lying on the rusty bed of the pickup, Saffy rolled about and wondered if the constant pitching gait of the vehicle would leave her covered with bruises. But she was willing to endure discomfort as the price of having escaped Zahir.

What on earth had come over her ex-husband? Their

marriage had been a train wreck and who in their right mind would want to revisit that?

And the answer came to her straight away. Failure of any kind was anathema to Zahir, whose callous old father had expected his son to excel in every field and who had punished him when he botched anything. Zahir was trying to rewrite the past. Why didn't he appreciate that that was impossible? People changed, people moved on...

Although she had not moved on very far, a tart little voice reminded Saffy, who was bitterly conscious that she was still a virgin. And time rolled back for her as she lay there and the pickup rattled and roared across the sands, threatening to shake her very teeth loose from her gums. Saffy had been eighteen and working at a department-store beauty counter when she first met Zahir. She hadn't wanted to go to university like her twin, had preferred to jump straight into work and start earning. Zahir had travelled to London with his sister, Hayat, who had been shopping for her wedding trousseau. Saffy still remembered seeing Zahir that very first time, her heart jumping inside her, her breath shortening as she collided with the most mesmerising dark golden eyes she had ever seen. Hayat had bought cosmetics while Saffy stared fixedly at Zahir and Zahir stared back equally transfixed at Saffy. She had never felt anything that powerful, either before then or since: an exhilarating and intrinsically terrifying instant attraction that swamped her like a fog, closing out the rest of the world and common sense.

'I will meet you after you finish work,' Zahir had told her in careful English.

He had told her that he was an army officer in Maraban. He hadn't told her that he was a prince or the son of the ruler of Maraban. She had had to look up Maraban online to find out where it was and her mother, Odette, with whom she had briefly lived at the time, had laughed at her and said, 'Why worry? He'll be gone in a few days and you'll never see him again.'

Initially Saffy had been desperately afraid of that forecast. After only a handful of dates, she had fallen for Zahir like a ton of bricks and she had been ecstatic when he told her he would be back the following month to attend a course at Sandhurst. She remembered little romantic snapshot moments from that period: sitting in a park below a cloud of cherry blossom with Zahir brushing a petal out of her hair with gentle fingers; lingering over coffee holding hands; laughing together at mime artists in the street. From the outset, Zahir had had the magic key to winning her trust, for, unlike previous boyfriends he didn't grab and grope and didn't expect her to leap straight into bed with him. At the same time, though, he was chary of the part-time modelling she was already doing, even when assured that she didn't do nude or underwear shots. She had recognised that he was old-fashioned in a way that had gone out of fashion in her country, but she had very much admired the seriousness of his quick clever mind and his unvarnished love for Maraban. Long before his course was over he asked her to marry him and he told her who he really was. And the news that he was a royal prince had merely added another intoxicating layer of sparkle to the fairy-tale fantasy she was already nourishing about their future together, Saffy conceded sadly.

Zahir had married her in a brief ceremony at the Marabani embassy without any of his family present and without his father's permission. With hindsight she knew how courageous he had been to wed her without his father's consent and she knew he had done it because he had known that his parent would never agree to him taking a foreign bride. Reality, unfortunately, hadn't entered their relationship until she landed in Maraban. Starting with the wedding night during which she panicked and threw up and ending with a daily life more like imprisonment than marriage, their relationship had hit the rocks fast. She hadn't been able to give him sex and neither of them had been able to handle the fallout from that giant elephant in the room. Any sense of intimacy had died fast, leading to backbiting conversations and even more of Zahir's constant absences.

The pickup came to a sudden jolting halt. A door slammed and a burst of voices met her straining ears. As the voices receded she began to snake out from below the tarpaulin, only then appreciating that it was almost dark. That was not a possibility she had factored into her plans and, climbing out of the truck, she soon recognised the second big drawback. It had not occurred to her that the driver might be rendezvousing with his family at a huge multi-roofed tent right out in the desert. Consternation swallowed Saffy whole as she stared round her at what she could see in the fast-fading light. There was no sign of a village, a road or anything else for her to focus on as a means of working out where she was. Biting her lip with vexation, she was pushing her bottle of water into the front pocket of her jeans when a tall pale shape clad in beige desert robes moved out of the tent.

'It's cold,' he said. 'Come inside.'

Disbelieving her ears, Saffy froze and gaped, her eyes straining to penetrate the growing darkness. '*Zahir?*' she exclaimed incredulously. 'What are you doing here?'

With one hand he tugged off the headdress bound with a gold and black circlet of cord and straightened, black hair ruffling back against his lean strong face in the slight breeze, his dark eyes bright as stars in the low light. 'I drove you here.'

'You...*what*?' Saffy gasped in disbelief.

'The security surveillance at the palace is the best money can buy,' Zahir drawled. 'I saw you climbing into the pickup on CCTV and I decided that if anyone was going to take you anywhere it should be me.'

'I've been under that tarpaulin for more than an hour!' Saffy launched at him in a rage of disbelief. 'I was so thrown about under it I'm not convinced my bones are still connected!'

Zahir shrugged without even a hint of sympathy. 'Well, it was your chosen mode of travel.'

'Don't you give me that!' Saffy flung at him through teeth that were starting to chatter because it was extraordinarily cold, but mercifully her temper was still rising like rocket fuel to power her. 'You knew I was in there!'

'Perhaps I thought a little shaking was a just reward for a woman stupid enough to climb into a car driven by a stranger when she didn't even know where the car was heading.'

Such a jolt of rage roared through Saffy that she was vaguely surprised that she didn't levitate into the air like a sorcerer. Her great blue eyes flashed. 'Don't you *dare* call me stupid!' she warned him in a hiss.

Zahir had never been the type to withdraw from a fight. He stood his ground, wide shoulders thrown back, stubborn jaw line set like granite. 'But it was *very* stupid to take such a risk with your personal safety.'

Saffy knotted her hands into fists and clenched her teeth together. 'My safety wouldn't be an issue if you hadn't kidnapped me!' she bit back.

'I kept you safe and I will continue to keep you safe and unharmed until you return to London because while you are here you are my responsibility,' Zahir countered in a tone of crushing finality. 'Now I suggest that you come inside so that you can wash and eat. I don't know about you…but I'm hungry.'

'Mr Practical…Mr Reasonable all of a sudden!' Saffy raged back at him, aggrieved by his unshakeable self-assurance in the face of her violent and perfectly reasonable resentment. 'How could you do this to me? I hate you! Get stuffed!'

Zahir expelled his breath in a slow sibilant hiss.

'When you are ready to be civil again, you may come inside and join me.'

And with that ultimate putdown, he was gone, striding soundlessly into the dimly lit tent and simply leaving her standing there. Saffy stamped her feet in the sand to express her fury and only just resisted an urge to slam her fists up against the metal side of the pickup. What a prune she felt—what a complete and utter idiot! Her bid for freedom had been seen and Zahir had stepped into the driver's seat to ruin her escape attempt. He had made a fool of her and not for the first time. It was many years since Saffy had been so angry, for in general she was the mildest personality around and quite laid back in temperament, but Zahir's dominant gene got to her every time. She gritted her teeth, stretched her aching back and legs and leant back against the pickup. Contrary to her every expectation of the desert, it was absolutely freezing and her tee was so thin she might as well have been naked. She couldn't stop shivering and she rubbed her chilled goose-fleshed arms in an effort to get her circulation going again. Seeing Zahir again seemed to have fried her brain cells.

When she couldn't stand the cold any longer she stalked into the tent, which was even larger than she had appreciated and even offered communicating doorways to other sections. Festooned in traditional kelims, it nonetheless offered sofas in place of the usual rugs round the fire pit. Zahir was being served coffee by a kneeling older man.

'What is this place?' Saffy asked abruptly. 'Where are we?'

'It's a semi-permanent camp where I meet with the tribal sheikhs on a regular basis. Although I know you would sooner be dead than sleep under canvas, it offers every comfort,' he murmured smoothly. 'The bathroom is through the second door.'

A wash of heated embarrassment engulfed Saffy's pale taut face. He was throwing her own words of five years ago back in her teeth, her less than tactful rejection of anything to do with tents and the nomadic lifestyle that had once been customary for his people.

'I suppose it's too much to hope that there's a shower in there?' Saffy breathed tautly.

'No, it is not. Go ahead and freshen up. A change of clothing has been laid out for you.'

Her gaze flickered uneasily off his darkly handsome features, her heart beating too fast for comfort or calm. Straight out of the frying pan right into the fire, she acknowledged uncomfortably as she brushed back the hanging that concealed a normal wooden door and stepped through it into a bathroom that contained every luxurious necessity. She stripped off in haste because even cold as she was she still felt sweaty and grubby, and her white linen trousers had not withstood the journey well. The powerful shower washed the grit from her skin and an impressive array of surprisingly familiar products greeted her on a shelf. Wrapped in a towel, she combed out her wet hair and made use of the hairdryer. Hot running water and electric in a tent?

Had he told her that that was a possibility she would have agreed to the desert trip he had tried to take her on soon after they were married. Or *would* she have? If she was honest, her fear of the intimacies of sharing a tent with him had lain behind her dogged refusal to consider such an excursion.

A silk kaftan lay over a chair with a pair of simple mules beside it. Leaving her underwear with her clothes, she slid into it, wondering what she would wear the following day and where he was planning for her to sleep. There were at least two more doorways leading out of the main tent for her to investigate.

'Are you ready to eat?' Zahir asked.

Eyes widening, she nodded affirmation and spun to look at him. He had shed the robes and got back into jeans. Damp black hair feathered round his lean bronzed features, accentuating those smouldering amber gold eyes surrounded by dense black lashes. Her pulses gave a jump. Butterflies flocked loose in her tummy and she swallowed hard, frantic to shed her desperate physical awareness of him. It seemed so schoolgirlish and immature to react that way after all the years they had been apart and the life she had since led. She was supposed to be calm, sophisticated…in control.

'No table and chairs, I'm afraid,' he warned her, settling down by the flickering fire with animal grace.

'That's OK,' she muttered as a servant emerged from one of the doorways bearing a tray, closely followed by another. 'So, you have a kitchen here.'

'A necessity when I'm entertaining.'

He had mentioned the tribal sheikhs he met up with but Saffy was already wondering how many other women he had brought out into the desert. She *knew* there had been other women. For a couple of years after the divorce and before the overthrow of his father, Zahir had made occasional appearances in glossy magazines with several different beautiful women on his arm. And those glimpses of the new and much more visible life he was leading abroad without her had cut deep like a knife and made her bleed internally. She had known that those women were sharing his bed, entangling his beautiful bronzed body with lissom limbs and giving him everything she had failed to give him. Divorce, she had learned the hard way, wasn't an immediate cut-off point for emotions, even emotions that she had no right to feel.

Zahir watched Sapphire curl up on the sofa opposite, looking all fresh faced and scrubbed clean just the way he remembered her, the way he liked her best, for with her stunning looks she required few enhancements. Her restive fingers toyed with a strand of golden blonde hair and instantly he recalled the silken feel of it sliding against his skin and got a hard-on. He crushed the recollection before it could stray into even more erotic areas and reminded himself that she was a beautiful shell with a cash-register heart. He was not at all surprised that she had dropped the subject of the five million pounds without any acknowledgement or adequate explanation. It might be pocket change to a member of his family, but it still mattered that she had taken so much and given nothing in return.

Perched with a plate on her lap, Saffy helped herself to portions of different dishes and dug in because she was starving. While she ate she studied Zahir from below her lashes, marvelling at the superb bone structure that gave his features such strength and masculinity. From every angle he was glorious. Sitting there, his attention on his plate and quite unaware of her scrutiny, he mesmerised her. Her breasts stirred beneath the silk, the tips growing tender and swollen. She dredged her eyes back to her food, her mouth dry, her heart hammering, images from the past bombarding her. Although consummating their marriage had proved impossible, she had learned how to give him pleasure in other ways. At that thought she shifted uneasily on her seat, moist heat pooling at the heart of her. He had never understood what was wrong with her. How could he have? But he had at least *tried,* assuring her of his patience while he did everything possible to set her fears to rest. Unfortunately her fears had been in her subconscious and not something she could control, fears from a hidden source that she had repressed many years before while she was still a child. All of a sudden she simply could not comprehend why he would bring her back into his life after a marriage that had turned into a hell on earth for both of them.

'Why on earth did you want to see me again?' Saffy demanded abruptly.

He lifted his dark head, stunning golden eyes locking to her. 'Few men forget their first love and you're the one who got away…'

Regret stabbed through her and she flinched, for they had begun with love in spite of the fact that during the year of marital strife that followed they had lost it again. The plates were cleared away and coffee and cakes served. She ate to fill the emptiness inside her, the hollow that never seemed to fill. She couldn't look at him, didn't dare look at him again, knew the temptation was a weakness to be suppressed at every opportunity.

'I wanted to see you again before I remarried,' Zahir heard himself admit in brusque addition, knowing that he would never have trusted himself to see her after that event had taken place.

Her golden head flew up, heavenly blue eyes wide with shock. 'You're getting married again?' she gasped, shattered at the idea although she couldn't have explained why.

Zahir raised a winged ebony brow. 'As yet there is no particular bride in view but there is considerable pressure on me to take a wife. Inevitably I will have to satisfy my people's expectations.'

Some of the tension eased from her taut shoulders and she lowered her head. Of course he would be expected to marry: it went with the territory of kingship. What did it matter to her? Why should the concept bother her? It was not as though she still thought of him as her husband. In fact she was being ridiculously oversensitive and it was time to grow up and don her big-girl pants. Exhaustion engulfed her in a debilitating wave then, reminding her that she had been up since five that morning. A yawn crept up on her and she stood up smothering a yawn. 'I'm incredibly tired…'

Zahir sprang upright and rested his hands on her shoulders to prevent her from moving away. Her mouth ran dry, her heart skipping a beat as she looked up at him, up over that full sensual mouth to the black-lashed golden eyes that wreaked havoc with her insides.

'Tonight you're tired.' His deep dark voice reverberated through her very bones, the husky nuances toying with her nerves like a secret caress. 'I won't touch you…'

Saffy shivered at just the thought of being in bed with him again. The image caught at her and not with the sense of threat that she believed she should have felt. A lazy brown forefinger grazed the length of her delicate collarbone, smoothed a passage up her slender throat while she struggled not to fall in a limp heap at his feet because her knees were threatening to buckle. She couldn't breathe, couldn't think while he touched her, and then he brought his mouth crashing down on hers with a hungry passion that should have frightened her out of her wits, but which instead stormed through her and set her on fire. There was a primitive sense of tightening and dampness between her legs, a sudden painful pulse throbbing through the peaks of her breasts. With every plunge of his tongue she trembled, lost in the hot, electrifying darkness of overwhelming physical sensation.

'Bed,' Zahir muttered raggedly, stooping to haul her up bodily in his strong arms, thrusting back a door with an impatient shoulder. 'I want you wide awake tomorrow.'

He laid her down on a big modern divan dressed in pristine white linen. When he had said, 'bed' in that deep thrilling tone her imagination had exploded into the stratosphere and when he released her again and moved back to the door, she frowned at him poised there in the dim light, black hair tousled by her fingers, the taste of him still on her lips, the sheer call of him to her senses overpowering. She rolled over and buried her hot face in a pillow. No, she didn't have a stupid bone in her body. She was looking for a man—had been for years— but he was not the one, although inconveniently he still seemed to be the *only* one she actually wanted, the only one she could even imagine becoming intimate with.

Angry tears of frustration stung her eyes. After the divorce had destroyed her faith in true love and happy endings, she had licked her wounds for years, terrified of getting into another serious relationship and meet- ing up with the same problems. But after therapy, she had longed to lose her virginity and have sex with a lover to prove that she was fully cured and had come to terms with her past. She had simply wanted to be *normal* as other women took for granted…how could that be wrong? Or selfish? Or immoral? And she did not need to compound her mistakes by being attracted to a man who had not only hurt her very badly once but who also had plans to marry another woman.

Zahir went for a shower—a very cold one. A great well of burning hunger was consuming him but it was cooled by disturbing memories of Sapphire shaking with unmistakeable fear when he had tried to make love to her during their marriage. Even with all the sexual experience he had painstakingly acquired since then, he was wary and seriously distrustful of the physically encouraging vibes she was putting out. He had been wrong before; why shouldn't he be wrong again? And while a faint sense of wonderment was stirring that he should actually have her in a bed again within reach, no sense of regret yet assailed him. In fact a merciless sense of all-male satisfaction was still driving him hard.

Saffy froze when she heard the door open again and rolled over, ridiculously conscious that her eyelids and her nose were probably pink from the overload of emotion and events that had brought overwrought tears to her eyes. She sat up in honest surprise to stare at Zahir, poised one step inside the door clad in only a pair of black silk boxers. Her throat closed over and she stopped breathing.

'There is only one bed...'

'It's not a problem,' Saffy responded as carelessly as she could contrive, rolling off the bed and yanking the bedspread off the mattress in almost the same movement. 'I'll sleep on the floor, although you *could* have taken one of the sofas.'

'I refuse to do so and you can't sleep on the floor.'

'I can do whatever I want to do,' Saffy told him, rolling herself into the spread and lying down beside the bed as well wrapped up as an Arctic explorer.

'Except when I'm around,' Zahir pronounced in direct challenge, snatching her up from the floor and planting her back on the divan with the strength that came so naturally to him.

'I'm not sharing that bed with you!' Saffy spat at him.

Zahir dealt her a derisive appraisal. 'Even when you already know that you can certainly trust me to hear the word no?' he queried in a very dry reminder.

Hot pink colour washed her lovely face and then receded to leave her pale and stricken. She was crushed by all that went unsaid within that aide-memoire, but equally suddenly she felt foolish making such a fuss about sharing a bed, and she squirmed out of the cloaking folds of the spread to slide below the sheet. 'This is all your fault—you should never have brought me here!'

Zahir almost laughed. She was shouting at him again, fighting with him, and he should have been furious at her lack of respect but he wasn't; he was too busy enjoying the novelty of being treated like an equal by a woman. Sapphire wouldn't bat her eyelashes at him, look down in submission and offer honeyed words of feminine flattery as the other women he met did. He climbed into the bed and lay back against the pillows. With Sapphire's mane of hair tossed all over the pillow beside his, the smell of the shampoo she used wafted into his nostrils, a familiar floral scent she had worn ever since he had known her, and that evocative aroma awakened too much that he would have preferred to forget. Slowly his lean brown hands clenched into fists, the tension in his lean powerful body extreme.

'Well, isn't this cosy?' Saffy mocked, determined not to show weakness again.

'Don't rock the boat...' Zahir purred softly in warning.

'Your English has improved so much,' Saffy remarked acidly, staring up at the boarded ceiling. 'Was that a by-product of your promiscuity with various Western women or did you actually have to study the language?'

His even white teeth gritted. The novelty of her backchat was fast dimming in appeal and he sat up to stare down at her. 'I was *not* promiscuous...'

Saffy stared stonily back at the lean bronzed beauty of his arresting face. 'None of my business.'

Eyes as dark a black and cold as she had ever seen them, he swivelled away from her and turned on his side and she caught a glimpse of his back, and anything else provocative that she might have said was forgotten instantly. Without thought she thrust down the sheet to get a better look. The once-brown silken sweep of his smooth, muscular back was marred with slashed and intersecting lines of scars. Before she could think better of it, she exclaimed, 'What on earth happened to your back?'

In an abrupt movement, Zahir flipped round to lie flat on his back again while colour crawled across his slashing cheekbones because he had forgotten to keep his shirt on. 'Not something I want to talk about.'

'But it looks like you were beaten...*whipped!*' Saffy burst out, unable to stifle her horror at the thought of anyone deliberately inflicting that amount of pain on him. His back must have been shredded to leave scars that deep and extensive.

In the nerve-racking silence, which only Zahir was capable of using like a weapon he switched out the light. She could recall so many times when he had shut her out like that five years earlier, keeping his own counsel, refusing to share his thoughts or even the details of what he did or where he went when he was away from her. He wasn't the confiding type, never had been, was very much made in the iron image of an army officer with the proverbial stiff upper lip. She compressed her lips on the questions tumbling on her tongue. Had he been caught, imprisoned and mistreated during the rebellion that had brought his father down? But surely his status as his father's heir should have protected him on either side of the fence?

Bewildered, even wondering why she should be so curious, Saffy closed her eyes and instead pictured him lounging in his boxers by the door and finally she smiled faintly in the darkness, the more disturbing images banished. He might have acquired a few scars but he was still a vision of bronzed masculine perfection, still her fantasy male from his perfect pecs to his six-pack abdomen and powerful hair-roughened thighs. He would either be highly amused or highly offended to learn that she pictured him when she tried to look sexy in a pose.

CHAPTER FOUR

SAFFY WOKE UP because she was too warm and then went rigid, for at some stage of the night she and Zahir had drifted across the great divide of mattress separating them in the huge bed and it was hardly surprising that she had overheated. Their bodies were welded together like two magnets and, compared to her, he put out the most extraordinary amount of heat. Even more disturbing, however, was the hard male arousal she could feel thrusting against her thigh.

He was always in that state in the morning: she had realised that while she was married to him. But the flush of awareness that shimmered through her was shockingly new, fresh and intensely energising and she shivered. Her fingers flexed against the male bicep they were resting on, colour flashing across her embarrassed face as a hunger to touch him flared deep inside her. It was a supreme irony that in the past, while she couldn't bear him to touch her, she had *loved* to touch him.

Black lashes dark as midnight and effective as silk fans swept up and she collided with stunning golden eyes and knew instantly what he was thinking. She

yanked her hand off his strong muscular bicep and
snaked back from him but she wasn't quick enough,
for Zahir had closed long brown fingers into her hair
to entrap her.

'Right at this minute,' he positively purred like a very
large predatory jungle cat on the prowl, 'I'm all yours.'

'I don't know what you're talking about!' she said in
desperation, a spasm of panic claiming her.

'Want me to tell you what you're thinking about?'
Zahir husked. 'Or will I just tell you what *I'm* thinking about?'

'Let me go!' she gasped.

He freed her hair and rolled back.

Low in her pelvis something clenched almost painfully while her nipples tingled into throbbing beads.

'You want me to take care of this myself?' He ges-
tured towards where his erection was evident beneath
the sheet, shameless in his enjoyment of her most mor-
tifying yet moment of recollection as if he had somehow
worked out exactly what was on her mind.

No, she wanted to flatten him to the bed, kiss her
way down the roped muscles of his stomach *and...* With
a stifled sound of distress, Saffy leapt off the bed as
though she had been bitten and fled from the room to
the bathroom. He had *kidnapped* her, deprived her of
her freedom and she had been lying there in that bed
tempted to reach for him, touch him, caress him with
her mouth, watch him reach a climax with pride and
satisfaction, the only satisfaction she had ever known in

the bedroom, an entirely one-sided stunted thing born of her inability to engage in intercourse.

He was cruel; no, he was gorgeous. She couldn't make her mind up to the extent that in the grip of that struggle she felt semi-insane and, refusing to think, she took care of her more pressing needs instead. A knock sounded on the door when she had finished brushing her teeth with the brand new battery-powered tooth-brush set out for her use. After a moment's hesitation, she yanked the door open. Sheathed in jeans and noth-ing else, Zahir handed her a pile of clothing.

'I was joking.'

'No, you weren't,' Saffy snapped.

Zahir lifted and dropped his lean brown hands and sudden amusement slashed his full sensual mouth. 'Well, I wouldn't have said no…first and foremost, I'm a man and I have some very hot memories of you.'

'H-hot?' Saffy stammered helplessly, taken aback by the word, certain he must have misused it.

Zahir stared at her, taking in the tousled golden hair hanging like a veil round her slim shoulders, the brighter than bright blue eyes, and acknowledged that the em-barrassment her entire stance telegraphed was not at all what he had expected from her. She wasn't an innocent any more, so why was she blushing?

'In that department you were very hot.'

Cold tainted her at the meaning of that sentence, the reminder that there had been others intimate with him since their divorce. 'Now that you can make com-parisons?'

'Don't take that angle—it's offensive,' Zahir ground out with sudden force. 'If I'd known what I was doing in our bed, we wouldn't have had problems!'

Consternation slivered through her taut length. 'Is that what you thought? That it was somehow *your* fault? You are so wrong, Zahir. There was nothing you could have done to make things any different between us,' she declared with fierce conviction, her innate sense of fairness making her speak up. 'I needed professional help.'

Saffy couldn't believe she was telling him her even a little piece of her biggest secret, but then he had been the only other person who had experienced her problems with her. It shook her that he had blamed his inexperience for *her* failure in the bedroom, but then how could he possibly have guessed what was really wrong with her? Was that why he had come up with the insane idea of kidnapping her? Was that why he still supposedly wanted her? Was that ferocious pride of his still set on rewriting the past and retrieving his masculine pride?

Zahir frowned, his surprise palpable. 'Professional help?'

'Never mind. Like you last night and your back... not something I choose to discuss,' Saffy fielded, because she was extremely reluctant to share her secrets, and indeed was already wondering if he might consider her in some way 'soiled' if he knew the truth. And just at that moment, quite ridiculously in the circumstances, she really *did* value the fact that, in spite of everything, Zahir was *still* attracted to her. It made her feel better about the past, and when she collided afresh with his mesmerising dark golden eyes she was beset by a stark sense of regret and loss. After all, when she stripped all the complications away one fact stood clear: he wanted her and she was still fiercely attracted to him, the guy she had fallen for as a teenager. Did that make her sad and pathetic? Was it the pull of first love that still made her want to reach out to him? Or simply that all-important element of sexual desire that she had not so far managed to find with another man?

And did it really matter? she asked herself, for at last the opportunity to move into the adult world and be a normal woman was being offered to her with no strings attached. If she had sex with Zahir, nobody would ever know about it and she would never see him again… Wasn't this finally the chance for her to achieve the intimacy that she had always longed to experience? Sex was a physical thing, she bargained with herself, and it didn't have to mean anything, didn't have to take place within a defined relationship. Her sister, Kat, was a bit of a prude and had raised her to have a very different outlook…but Saffy had done the serious thing, the marriage thing and the love thing and had ended up broken to pieces inside herself, enduring a pain and insecurity that she had still not managed to overcome. Simple sex would be enough for her, she reasoned in desperation, suppressing her uneasy feelings while telling herself that she was surely old enough and mature enough to follow her own instincts.

'Go back to bed,' Saffy murmured tautly, the momentous decision already made and it was a choice that she felt she could live with. 'I'll join you in a few minutes…'

Zahir's cloaking black lashes lifted on frowning dark eyes of incomprehension. 'What are you saying?'

Saffy shrugged a slender shoulder, putting on a face because her pride was too great to allow him to suspect how insecure and inexperienced she actually was. 'It's only sex, not something worth making a fuss about…'

Taken aback by that blunt statement, Zahir breathed in deep. 'Passion is always worth pursuing.'

'Not in my world,' Saffy countered doggedly, thinking of the many casual affairs she had seen begin and end among her friends, and she doubted that true passion-ripping-your-clothes-off passion—had driven many of them. Loneliness and lust would be a more honest description of their motivation.

Zahir stepped forward, lean brown hands reaching up to curve to her cheekbones and centre her gaze on him. 'If that's true, I find it sad. I want to give you passion.'

'No, you don't,' she whispered. 'You said it yourself. I'm the one who got away and you can't live with that.'

'It's not that simple,' Zahir growled, protest etched in every hard, angular line of his powerful bone structure while he clashed with her beautiful blue eyes, knowing that no other eyes had ever been so very deep a blue that they reminded him of the sky on a hot summer day.

'Don't make it complicated,' she urged, her breath hitching as he angled down his tousled dark head and her lips tingled like a silent invitation.

'It was always complicated with us,' Zahir argued, stubborn to the last.

And Saffy rose up on her toes and angled her lips up to his, eager to stop him talking and treading all over her memories with hob-nailed boots in that obstinate, all-male, infuriating way of his. He kissed her and her heart seemed to jolt to a sudden halt inside her chest. He stole her breath with a kiss of such unashamed passion that she felt light-headed and her legs went weak.

He carried her back to bed, yes, *carried,* her bemused mind savoured, for very few men were physically big enough or strong enough to lift five-foot-ten-inch Saffy off her feet as if she were of tiny and delicate proportions. He captured her mouth again with intoxicating urgency, his tongue delving deep between her lips, and her body sang. Even while doubts and fears about how she would react to what came next were circulating madly in the back of her head, she could feel the supersensitive awareness of desire infiltrating her, sending prickling spasms of warmth across her breasts and a kick of heat down into her pelvis.

'I assumed I would have to seduce you,' Zahir admitted, staring down at her with those amazing eyes and the kind of honesty she had once loved him for.

'It's no big deal,' Saffy countered a tad shakily, wondering if he would assume that she was a slut, always up for the possibility of a little fling with an attractive man when she was on her travels. But what did it matter what *he* thought? she demanded angrily of herself, because what she was planning to do was entirely for her own benefit and nothing whatsoever to do with him. That he would also be getting what he apparently wanted was only an accidental by-product of her decision. She was the one in control, *full* control. This was sex, nothing to do with the softer emotions, because she simply refused to let him screw up her emotions again.

Taken aback by that statement, Zahir frowned again, ebony brows drawing together.

'Call a spade a spade, Zahir!' Saffy snapped, out of all patience. 'Isn't this why you brought me here?'

'You've changed,' he condemned.

'Of course I have…I grew up, realised fairies and unicorns didn't exist, got divorced,' Saffy recited tightly.

And then he kissed her again, his mouth crashing down on hers with angry fervour and, even though she recognised the anger, she was exhilarated by his passion. He tugged her up into a sitting position and before she even knew what he was about he had swept the kaftan off over her head, leaving her naked but for the cloaking veil of her long blonde hair.

'You're still the most beautiful woman I've ever known,' Zahir declared.

And she still wasn't comfortable being naked around him, Saffy registered in dismay, fearful that the embarrassment enveloping her was only a small taster of the discomfiture she had felt in the past with her own body. Casual nudity was the norm behind the scenes at catwalk shows where fast changes of clothing were a necessity and that didn't bother her, but being naked in front of Zahir bothered her on a much more visceral level.

As he studied her a veil of hot red colour blossomed on her skin in a flush that ran from her breasts to her brow.

Long brown fingers lifted to the rounded perfection of pale breasts topped with distended pink nipples and he stroked the tightly beaded tips before he pushed her gently back against the pillows and bent his tousled dark head to put his sensual mouth there instead, suckling at the straining peaks until she gasped for breathe, shaken by even what she recognised to be a relatively minor intimacy. Even so, it was an intimacy that sent arrows of fire hurtling to her womb and her thighs trembled at the thought of what was yet to come. Let it be all right this time, she pleaded inside her head, snapping her eyes shut, seeking to blank out her thoughts lest the old panic take hold of her again.

Zahir couldn't quite believe that this was Sapphire, lying there, admittedly passive but not freaking out. It felt just a little like all his fantasies rolling up in one go and that disturbed him. He didn't know what he had expected and could only recognise how much she had changed while wondering with dark, forbidding fury which of her men had succeeded where he had so comprehensively failed. That mystery burned through his bloodstream like acid and he had to fight it, suppress it and exert iron control not to ask questions and demand answers. On the other hand, what if she was acting like a human sacrifice because that was how she felt?

He tasted her lush mouth with driving hunger, tried and failed to squash that inner question and lifted his head again. 'If you don't want this, tell me,' he told her.

Consternation filled Saffy to overflowing as she registered that evidently she wasn't putting on a very good impression of being a relaxed and experienced lover. She sat up with a start, her pale hands fixing to his smooth bronzed shoulders, blue eyes wide. 'I want this…I want you.'

'Then touch me,' he growled low in his throat, his hunger unconcealed in his star-bright gaze.

And on the edge of fright and uncertainty, she did, smoothing her hands over his warm golden skin, feeling the rope of muscles beneath his hard, flat stomach and his sudden driving tension as she found him with her fingers. Hard and silky and so velvety smooth and large. She gulped at the very thought of what he was going to do with it…*if* she managed—and she *had* to manage, had to be normal for the sake of her own sanity and his.

Zahir groaned with unashamed sensuality, lying back against the pillows, his black hair in stark contrast to the pale linen, eyes half closed and screened by his outrageous black lashes. 'Not too much,' he warned her unevenly. 'I'm too aroused.'

So, she stayed with the touching, her hand trembling slightly while she felt her body progressively warm in a great surging wash of desire. She needed him to touch her, needed that so badly that it hurt yet she was terrified that she might lose her nerve, her control. He hooked a long thigh over hers, nudging her legs apart, and she stopped breathing as if she were a candle being snuffed out, for this was the acid test, the one she couldn't really call and couldn't afford to fail. Long brown fingers smoothed down her thigh as if he knew on some level that, even hungry as she was, she was scared as no adult woman should be scared. After all, it wasn't as though he had ever physically hurt her. She regulated her breathing, cleared her head of such dangerous thoughts, for thinking that way was surely like inviting her phobia back in. He skated through the crisp golden curls on her mound and she bit her tongue so badly she tasted blood in her mouth and she was trembling, all hyped up with expectation, wanting and not wanting in that moment to test her boundaries. *New* boundaries, she reminded herself resolutely.

He kissed her again and she squirmed against him, insanely conscious of that exploring hand touching where she had never been touched in adult memory, rubbing over that wildly sensitive little button that she hadn't even known existed for more years than she cared to recall. Sensation sparked through her, startling in its very intensity, sending another cloud of heat through her quivering length. Before she even guessed what he was about to do, he eased a finger into her and she didn't go off into a panic attack, didn't jackknife back from him as though he had assaulted her. It felt strange to be touched like that, by someone else rather than by herself, but it didn't hurt and it didn't make her feel sick or frightened, and hope rose in a heady gush inside her that she was going to be all right, after all, and the scene was not set for another disaster.

With so much frantic reflection taking place inside her head, it took a minute at least for Saffy to register that she *liked* what he was doing, the sweet rise of sensation fanning through her lower body as his mouth toyed with an achingly sensitive nipple and his fingers delved into the tender wetness of her body. She hadn't expected to like it, she acknowledged, had simply regarded it as something she had to get through, the mountain of her virginal state at nearly twenty-four years of age a complex challenge that had to be conquered solely for her own benefit.

'I want you so much but you're very tight, *aziz*.' Zahir groaned, snaking down her body, and she didn't know what he was doing and almost yelped in dismay when he put his carnal mouth between her parted thighs instead, caressing the sensitive pink folds of her femininity.

Saffy lay there like a stone dropped to the bottom of a very deep well, so far out of her depth she felt lost, indeed shattered by the gathering waves of increasingly powerful sensation that he was wringing from her untried body. The wave gathered her up and kept on pushing her higher until she was pulsing and throbbing and aching with an excitement that she had never known existed. Her hips were rising, her back was arching and then suddenly, with very little warning, the instant she had most feared was there: his bold shaft was nudging against her for penetration and she tensed, struggling not to freeze, but every skin cell in her body was gripped by nerves that her body might bottle out and let her down at the worst and most unforgivable moment.

And then she experienced the delicious friction of his entry eased by the slick dampness of her arousal.

He was pushing, stretching her inner sheath with the hard, demanding pressure of his entrance and she was briefly amazed at what he felt like inside her. Instinctively she lifted her pelvis and he plunged forward and then it was done, a sharp stinging pain flashing through her so that her eyes widened and she gritted her teeth together, contriving to rein back a cry of pain. She pushed her face up into his shoulder to further conceal her reaction. He had no entitlement to the privilege of learning that, against all odds, he had become her first lover, and there was not much she would not have withstood to keep him from that knowledge. On that ungenerous thought a spasm of intense pleasure took her quite by surprise as her inner muscles tightened their grip on his intrusion.

With a low growl of satisfaction that vibrated his chest against her soft breasts, he began to move, pulling out, pushing back in. The strange seductive sensations built and she gasped, feeling her control sliding against the onslaught of a wild excitement she hadn't anticipated. Excitement roared through her, her heart hammering while she panted for breath. He lifted her legs over his shoulders, rising up over her like a conquering god, his lean darkly handsome face flushed and taut with driving desire and uninhibited satisfaction while he drove into her hard and fast with a pagan rhythm that put her every sense on overload.

Nothing had ever felt so good or so necessary to her. Had he stopped she would have screamed. He touched the tiny button below her mound again, rubbing fast, and the golden light already expanding inside her burst through into brilliance and exploded in a series of violent aftershocks throughout her body. The waves of hot, sweet pleasure racked her with compulsive shivers of disbelief and a certain amount of awe, for she had never dreamt that he might make her feel so much. He shuddered over her with a moan of intense masculine satisfaction and then fell still, letting her legs fall back down on the bed and rolling off her to pull her close.

'That was absolutely amazing,' Zahir breathed, his diction ragged, his accent pronounced, his chest still heaving against her as he pulled her close, their bodies damp with perspiration and sliding against each other.

But Saffy's sense of perfect peace lasted for only a few seconds. What struck her as *most* amazing at that moment was how much other women must have taught him, how much practice he must have had in other beds to have gained the sexual expertise he had just demonstrated. That fast she wanted to thump him hard and kick him out of bed and her hands knotted into fists of restraint below the sheet. Careful, she told herself in fierce and bemused rebuke, for she didn't recognise the feelings bombarding her. He was her ex-husband, not her lover, and she wasn't jealous or possessive where he was concerned. He meant absolutely nothing to her and she didn't understand why he was still holding her and pressing a kiss to her delicate jaw bone as though they had shared something special. After all, she had just used him to have sex for the first time and he had been good...well, *amazing,* to borrow his word. But that was an acknowledgement that only made her fists knot tighter and her temper flare even higher, for nothing could have been more different from the tentative and inexperienced young husband she remembered than the uninhibited demonstration of raunchy sex he had just treated her to.

Without hesitation, indeed reacting on pure gut instinct, Saffy pulled free of Zahir and slid off the bed in one strong movement, a mane of rumpled golden hair falling round her pale slender length like a veil. 'Do I qualify for a car to the airport now?' she asked thinly, blue eyes cold as the polar wastes.

Raking long brown fingers through his black hair, Zahir sat up in the tangled sheets, the white linen providing a striking foil for his golden skin. He tensed and swore and, assuming his reaction was the result of her sudden exit from the intimacy of the bed, she flicked him a bitter glance. Yes, he was still unquestionably gorgeous, but she hated him, totally hated him, wanted to be gone now as fast as possible, escaping the scene of the crime. No doubt he thought *he* had used her but it was the other way round and she would have liked the freedom to tell him that, but was still not prepared to spill her deepest secrets to him.

'I want you to stay until tomorrow,' Zahir admitted in a low-pitched tone evocative of anticipation.

Her blue eyes flashed. 'No. I'm done here. I want to go home right now.'

Zahir, gloriously unaccustomed to being in receipt of a negative female response since his divorce, stared back at her with faint but perceptible hauteur while he wondered what had gone wrong. 'I don't do one-nighters.'

Her lovely face without expression, Saffy dealt him an impatient glance, eyes as unemotional as stones. 'I do and, as I said, I'm done.'

Determined not to meet his gaze, Saffy focused on the neat pile of freshly laundered clothes sitting on a chair and wondered when they had arrived, where they had contrived to get washed and ironed and when they had been returned, for all of those inconsequential thoughts were safer than thinking about the insane passion she had just shared with Zahir. She scooped her clothes up and headed at a brisk pace for the bathroom.

Zahir leapt out of bed and reached the door a step ahead of her, one brown hand bracing on the door to keep it shut. 'There's something I should tell you first.'

Refusing to look directly at him, Saffy grimaced. 'What?' she asked impatiently.

'The condom I used broke…I suspect I was too passionate. I assume that you're on the contraceptive pill and that there's no risk of conception?' he pressed with the evident belief that that was the natural order for a woman like her.

For a split second her eyes narrowed and she paled as she assimilated that shocking information, suddenly grasping what had most probably provoked his curse mere minutes earlier, and although a chill of dismay gripped her she nodded immediate agreement. 'Of course,' she lied, wanting him to believe that she was already taking that precaution against pregnancy because she slept with other men, for that belief best conserved her pride. And she also knew how much that belief would annoy him…for he was possessive to his backbone. At least, he *had* been when she knew him, she qualified grimly, but who could say what drove him now? Five years' separation, a lot of other women and possession of a throne had changed him: of course, they had. It would be very naïve of her to think otherwise.

'I'll organise transport,' Zahir breathed grittily. 'And see that the film shot of the commercial is also delivered to you before you depart.'

'Is that my reward?' Saffy enquired drily, concealing her relief that he was willing to hand over the film, well aware that the film crew and her clients would be going mad over its confiscation.

His handsome features clenched. 'If you choose to see it that way—'

'Oh, I do,' Saffy asserted, watching gold glimmer like a flame in his dark as midnight eyes and loving the burn of it, knowing she had annoyed him as he threw open the door for her to leave the bedroom section of the tent. 'And while I remember it, I would advise you to look more closely into the disappearance of that five million pounds you mentioned—because I'm telling you now, I didn't receive a penny of it!'

Zahir inclined his arrogant dark head in grudging acknowledgement. 'I will have the matter investigated,' he conceded, coldly formal in tone.

Was he offended that she hadn't appeared to want a repeat of their intimacy? Saffy stepped into the shower and washed her skin clean of the scent of him. She felt sore, every movement of her lower limbs reminding her of his passionate possession. It was done. She was no longer a virgin. She had surmounted her fears. She was *finally* a normal young woman and now in a condition to consider a relationship as a potential part of her future. That was good, she told herself firmly. She forced her stiff facial muscles into a determined smile and had just wrapped a towel round her dripping body when a knock sounded on the door and heralded Zahir's reappearance, his lean bronzed body still clad only in boxer shorts.

'Yes?' Saffy prompted tightly, not having wanted to see him again because seeing him hurt, made her think of the other women he had been with and, even though it wasn't fair or even rational when she had been unable to consummate their marriage while they were together and they were now divorced, she hated him for having found pleasure and satisfaction when she could not.

'I must have hurt you…there's spots of blood on the sheet,' Zahir informed her grimly. 'Why didn't you tell me?'

Hot colour flew into her cheeks like a banner of scarlet. It had not occurred to her that there might be any detectable physical proof of her innocence and she was mortified by his discovery. 'You didn't hurt me…er, it's been a while for me, so perhaps that explains it,' she muttered awkwardly through clenched teeth of discomfiture.

'Why has it been a while for you?' Zahir demanded bluntly. 'You live with a man.'

Somehow he contrived to voice that statement in a manner and tone that implied she regularly sold her body on street corners. 'That's my business,' Saffy responded flatly, her eyes veiled.

'You should see a doctor,' Zahir informed her curtly. 'I can contact someone—'

'No, thanks.' Her cup of humiliation now truly running over and threatening to drown her, Saffy moved towards him and opened the door for his exit. 'Excuse me, I'd like to get dressed.'

'Sapphire…' Frustration stamped on his lean dark features, Zahir glowered down at her, smouldering golden eyes alight. 'Why are you behaving like this? Is this a habit of yours? Do you often indulge in casual sex?'

She refused to look at him and her lush mouth compressed so hard that her lips turned bloodless. 'That would be kissing and telling, which I definitely *don't* do.'

CHAPTER FIVE

SAFFY RESTED BACK in her cream leather reclining seat
in Zahir's incredibly opulent private jet, but beneath the
skin her every muscle was tense and she could not relax.

Even so, Zahir had certainly ensured that she was
travelling back to London in style. She frowned at the
acknowledgement because she would have preferred
to consign every image and conversation of the past
twenty-four hours to a mental dustbin sealed with a good
strong lid. She had slept with her ex, no big deal, she told
herself with rigorous resolve. It was only a major event
for her because having sex had been something she had,
until relatively recently, been afraid she couldn't ever
do. *She* had used *him*. That was how she had to look on
what had happened. If he knew that his temper would
have gone nuclear because Zahir expected everything
on his own terms. In that spirit he had married her and
in the same spirit he had decided to divorce her again.
Nothing had ever been equitably discussed: he had been
happy to make his mind up for both of them.

Five years ago, they had landed in Maraban as a
newly married couple and that too had been very much

on his terms, with her not having the first clue about the dysfunctional royal family she had joined. His father, King Fareed, had been livid that his younger son had married a foreigner and had initially refused to even meet her. She had met Zahir's older brother, Omar, and his wife, Azel. Omar had died in a car crash a few months after Saffy arrived. As Omar and his wife had been childless, Zahir's importance to his father had mushroomed once he became the heir-in-waiting and Saffy had seen even less of her husband as he was forced to take on the ceremonial roles that had once been his brother's.

Staying in the royal palace just outside the city limits, Saffy had been sentenced to a very boring and hidden existence. As her father-in-law refused to accept her as part of the family and was determined to keep the presence of a Western blonde in the palace a secret, she had not been allowed to go out and about in Maraban and explore freely. Indeed aside of a few stolen shopping expeditions in the company of her widowed sister-in-law, Azel, Saffy had barely gone out at all. Zahir had declared that *eventually* his father would accept her as his wife but that she would have to be patient. But twelve months living like the invisible woman had convinced Saffy that her marriage had been a major mistake, particularly when things between her and Zahir had gone badly awry as well.

'You're very unhappy here,' Zahir had acknowledged the very last time she saw him during their marriage.

'You've been telling me that you wanted a divorce for the past six months and now I must agree.'

'Just like that you *suddenly* agree?' Saffy had yelled at him incredulously, shock at his change of heart winging through her in sickening waves as she realised he had clearly had enough of her and their marriage. 'But you swore that you still loved me, that we could work it out…'

'But now I want you to go home to London as soon as it can be arranged. I want to divorce you and set you free,' Zahir had countered as stonily as though she had not spoken.

It was true that for weeks whenever they argued she had hurled the threat of a divorce at him on a fairly frequent basis. But she had never really *meant* it, had simply been dramatising herself and struggling to make her young husband take her unhappiness seriously. But she had somehow still expected Zahir to continue to refuse to even consider divorce as the answer to their problems. Coming at her out of the blue like that, his volte-face had shocked her and pleading in the face of his clear determination to get rid of her had been more than she could bear. For so long, regardless of their difficulties, she had clung to her conviction that Zahir still loved her no matter what and that what they had together was still worth fighting for. Deprived of that consolation and cruelly rejected by the divorce that swiftly followed, Saffy had been heartbroken and not surprisingly had felt abandoned.

Her older sister, Kat, who had raised her from the

age of twelve, had tried to comfort Saffy, pointing out that King Fareed's opposition to their marriage must finally have worn Zahir down while reminding Saffy that neither she nor Zahir had foreseen the very real difficulties that would arise in Saffy's struggle to adapt to life in a different country, far from family and friends. Saffy didn't want to remember how appallingly she had missed Zahir after she left Maraban or how many months had passed before she could enjoy the freedom she had reclaimed and stop thinking about Zahir at least once every minute. She had genuinely loved him and it hurt to appreciate that he had moved on from her so much more easily than she had moved on from him. Maybe he had never really loved her, Saffy conceded painfully. Maybe it had *always* been about the sex and only the sex. Certainly, given his behaviour in shipping her out to the desert for seduction, that looked like the most viable explanation. It was equally agonising to admit that had she been capable of doing what she had just done with him five years earlier they might still have been together. Or *would* they have been? Was that just fantasy land? Perhaps all along she had only been a fling in the form of a wife for Zahir.

But didn't she have rather more pressing concerns in the present? What about that contraceptive accident they had had? Saffy tensed, her appetite evaporating in front of the beautiful lunch she had been served as her skin chilled with complete fright at the idea of being faced with an unplanned pregnancy. Once she had believed she would never have children because she wasn't able to have sex or even handle the concept of artificial insemination. Now she knew differently and knew her future had opened up another avenue once barred to her. So, if she did fall pregnant, what would she do about it? She had friends who would rush to request the morning-after pill after such a mishap to ensure that no conception took place, but if against all the odds new life did begin inside her, Saffy registered that she was totally unwilling to consider a termination. In that moment she was suddenly realising with a heart that felt full enough to burst that a baby would mean the sun, the moon and the stars to her and that there was nothing she would cherish more. It might be a disaster as far as her current clients were concerned, but it would only be a short-term one and surely her earning power wouldn't die overnight. She breathed in deep and slow, both terrified and enervated by the risk she was prepared to take with her own body. If conception happened, she decided, it would happen and she would embrace it without regret.

Having dropped off the film of the shoot with the exceedingly relieved production company, Saffy caught the tube back to the two-bedroom apartment she had bought with Cameron. Cameron, a keen cook, was in the kitchen dicing vegetables, but it was the sight of the small brunette perched on the counter chatting nineteen to the dozen to him that startled Saffy.

'*Saffy!*' Topsy cried, velvety somber eyes full of warmth as she leapt off the counter like a miniature whirlwind and threw herself exuberantly into her much taller sister's arms. At slightly less than four feet eleven inches tall, Topsy was tiny. 'I wish you hadn't been away this week. I wanted to go out with you to celebrate the end of my exams!'

Saffy's eyes stung as she gratefully accepted her youngest sister's affectionate hug. Topsy always wore her feelings on her sleeve. At eighteen years of age, having just finished school, Topsy was much less damaged by their disturbed childhood and more outgoing than her older sisters. She was also exceptionally clever and overflowing with an irrepressible joie de vivre that few could resist. Yet as Saffy studied the younger woman she saw shadows below her eyes and a tension far removed from Topsy's usual laid-back vibe and she wondered what was wrong.

'How did you find out that I was back so quickly?' Saffy prompted.

'She's been phoning here every day…I texted her after you called me from the airport,' Cameron, a tall attractive man with close-cropped dark curls, told her from his position by the state-of-the-art cooker.

'I assumed you'd want to stay on at Kat's with Emmie,' Saffy remarked.

'No, Kat and Mikhail are hosting a big dinner tonight and I wasn't in the mood to play nice with loads of strangers,' Topsy confided with a slightly guilty wince. 'And Emmie has already gone home again.'

Saffy's heart sank at that news because it was obvious to her that once again her twin had chosen to dodge meeting her. Her estranged twin was *still* avoiding her, Saffy acknowledged unhappily, wounded by Emmie's reluctance to even be in her company. Was she that bad? Was she truly so hateful to her twin? Or was it a simple if unpalatable fact that her past sins were beyond forgiveness?

'Emmie's gone back to Birkside?' she checked, referring to Kat's former home in the Lake District, the farmhouse her elder sister had inherited from her late father.

Kat was the daughter of their mother Odette's first marriage, the twins the daughters of her second marital foray while Topsy was the result of their mother's short-lived liaison with a South American polo player. By the time the twins reached twelve years of age they were a handful and Odette had placed all three girls in foster care. Kat, then in her twenties, had made a home at Birkside for all three of her sisters and Odette had had very little to do with her children since then. In every way that mattered, Kat had become the loving, caring mother her sisters had never really had.

'*Should* Emmie be on her own up there?' Saffy questioned the younger woman anxiously. 'I mean, it's a lonely house and now that she's pregnant…?'

Topsy rolled her eyes. 'Emmie always does her own thing and she has friends up there and a job,' she pointed out breezily. 'I also think that just at the minute Kat and Mikhail being so lovey-dovey makes them hard for Emmie to be around.'

Even while Saffy adored the fact that Kat had found happiness with a man who so obviously loved her, she too had felt like a gooseberry more than once in the couple's company. If her twin's solo pregnancy was the result of a recent relationship breakdown, Emmie was probably feeling a great deal more sensitive to that loving ambiance.

'Dinner will be ready in ten minutes,' Cameron announced.

'I've got time to get changed, then?'

'Yes. Let's go into your room,' Topsy urged, tugging at Saffy's arm.

A frown indented Saffy's brow at her sister's obvious eagerness to get her alone. 'What's up?' she asked as she closed her bedroom door.

Topsy, all liveliness sliding from her expressive face, sank down on the edge of the bed, hunched her shoulders and muttered, 'I found out something I wasn't prepared for this week and I didn't want to bother Kat with it,' she admitted.

Saffy dropped down on the stool by the dressing table. 'Tell me…'

'You'll probably think it's really silly,' Topsy confided.

'If it's upset you, it's not silly,' Saffy declared staunchly.

Topsy pulled a face. 'I don't know if I am upset. I don't know how I feel about it—'

'How you feel about what?' Saffy prompted patiently.

'A few weeks ago, my dad, Paulo, asked me to agree to a DNA test. I'm eighteen. We didn't need Kat's permission,' Topsy explained as Saffy raised her brows in astonishment at the admission. 'Apparently Dad had always had doubts that I was his child and since he got married he and his wife have had difficulty conceiving—'

'Your dad's got married? Since when? You never told us that!' Saffy exclaimed.

Topsy sighed. 'It didn't seem important. I mean, I've only met him a half-dozen times in my whole life. With him living in Brazil, it's not like we ever had the chance to get close,' she pointed out ruefully. 'Anyway, his new wife and him went for testing when she didn't fall pregnant and it turns out he's sterile.'

Saffy stiffened at the news. 'Hence the DNA testing...'

'And it turns out that I couldn't possibly be his kid,' Topsy confided with a valiant smile. 'So, I went to see Mum—'

Saffy gave her a look of dismay, for Odette was a challenging and devious personality. 'Please tell me you didn't!'

'Well, she was the only possible person I could approach on the score of my parentage,' Topsy pointed out ruefully. 'First of all she tried to argue that in spite of the DNA evidence I *was* Paulo's kid—'

'I doubt if she wanted the subject dug up after this length of time,' Saffy remarked stiffly, cursing their irresponsible and selfish mother and hoping she had dealt kindly with her youngest daughter.

'She definitely didn't,' Topsy admitted with a grimace of remembrance. 'She just said that if Paulo wasn't my father, she didn't know who was. Did she really sleep with that many men that she wouldn't know, Saffy?'

Saffy reddened and veiled her eyes. 'There were periods in her life when she was very promiscuous. I'm sorry, Topsy. That was an upsetting thing for you to find out. How did Paulo react?'

'I think he had already guessed. He didn't seem surprised. Let's face it, I don't look the slightest bit like him. He's over six foot tall and built like a rugby player,' Topsy reminded her companion ruefully. 'Now I'll probably never find out who my father is but why should that matter to me? After all, you and Emmie have a father who lives right here in London but who still takes no interest in you.'

Saffy groaned. 'That's different. Mum and him had a very bitter divorce. She dumped him because he lost all his money. When he built a new life and remarried and had a second family he didn't want anything more to do with us.'

'Does that bother you?'

'No, not at all. You can't miss what you've never had,' Saffy lied, for that was another rejection that still burned below the layer of emotional scar tissue she had formed. When she and her twin had been at their lowest ebb, their father, just like their mother, had turned his back on them and had said he wanted nothing to do with them.

'You're evil...just like your mother. Look what you've done to your sister!' he had told Saffy when she was twelve years old, and even the passage of time hadn't erased her memory of the look of dislike and condemnation in his gaze.

'Sorry to land you with all this,' her kid sister muttered guiltily.

Beyond the door Cameron called them for dinner and Saffy seized the chance to give her kid sister a comforting hug, wishing she had some clever reassurance to offer Topsy on the topic of absent father figures. Unfortunately, not having normal caring parents left a hole inside you and even Kat's praiseworthy efforts to fill that hole for her sisters had not proved entirely successful. Saffy had simply learned that when bad things happened you had to soldier on, hide your pain and deal with the consequences in private.

Only when Topsy had returned to Kat and Mikhail's home for the night with her spirits much improved did Cameron turn with a concerned look in his shrewd eyes to ask Saffy suspiciously, 'What—or should I say *who*—kept you unavoidably detained in Maraban?'

Saffy visibly lost colour. 'It's not something I want to talk about right now.'

'You know that's not a healthy attitude,' Cameron, who was a firm believer in therapy, warned her.

'Talking about anything personal will never come easily to me,' Saffy admitted tightly. 'I spent too many years locking everything up inside me.'

She was extraordinarily tired and she went to bed and lay there with her eyes wide open in the darkness, struggling to suppress the images of Zahir stuck inside her head. Fighting thoughts teemed alongside those unwelcome images. She would get over that little desert rendezvous in Maraban and leave Zahir behind her... in the past where he truly belonged.

* * *

Ten days later, Saffy wakened because while she had slept she had slid over onto her tummy and her breasts were too tender to withstand that pressure. With a wince, she sat up, wondering if it was time to use the pregnancy kit she had bought forty-eight hours earlier, but she was still strangely reluctant to put her suspicions to the test. Could she have enjoyed intimacy just one time and conceived when her unfortunate sister, Kat, had been trying without success to fall pregnant for many months? It struck her as unlikely and she had only bought the test in a weak moment of dreaming about what it might be like to become a mother.

Such silly dreams, *childish* dreams for a grown woman to be indulging in, she scolded herself impatiently, dreams full of fluffy, fantasy baby images and not a jot of reality. Somewhere deep down inside her a voice was telling her that a baby would be one little piece of Zahir that she could have and cherish, but she was intelligent enough to know that the reality of single parenthood was sleepless nights, cash worries and nobody else to share your worries and responsibilities with. Frustrated by her own rebellious brain, she got up and did her morning exercises, desperate to think of something else. When that didn't work she changed into her sports gear and went out for a run, returning to the apartment drenched in perspiration and on legs wobbly from over-exertion. Stripping, she walked into the shower and washed. She was towelling herself dry when she heard the doorbell buzz. She pulled on her robe and padded across the hall to answer.

She looked through the peephole first and froze, looked again, her heart rate kicking up a storm. *Zahir?* Here in London? Her teeth gritting, she undid the chain and opened the door.

'What do you want?' she demanded sharply.

CHAPTER SIX

'INVITE ME IN,' Zahir commanded.

Saffy was uneasily aware of the two security men standing by the lift, of the status and level of protection Zahir now required as the ruler of Maraban, and the very idea that he was now at risk of becoming a target for attack gave her stomach a sick jolt. She swallowed hard, mustering her defences such as they were. 'No.'

'Don't be juvenile,' Zahir urged, his handsome mouth tightening, his air of gravity lending a forbidding edge to the smooth planes of his lean dark absolutely gorgeous face. 'We have business to discuss.'

'*Business?*' Saffy parroted, suddenly wishing she hadn't opened the door with wet hair and a face bare of make-up for, deprived of her professional grooming, she felt defenceless.

'I told you that I would investigate the trust fund I set up for you.' Impatience edged his dark deep drawl, energised his stunning dark deep-set eyes with sparks of gold, and as she watched him her mouth ran dry as a bone. 'I have now done so.'

'Oh, the missing money,' she muttered in weak comprehension, and she stepped back with stiff reluctance to open the door, for she didn't want him inside her personal space, didn't want one more memory or association with him to further colour her existence.

'Yes, the money,' Zahir said drily, in a tone that suggested that he could have no other reason to roll up on her doorstep.

She studied him, in a split second memorising sufficient to commemorate his image for life, and she turned away, colour crawling up painfully over her cheekbones as she led the way into the living room. He wore a business suit, a beautifully tailored designer effort that showcased his height and breadth and long powerful legs. He had had his hair cut since she had last seen him, jet black hair feathering back from lean strong features to brush the collar of his shirt, the inevitable stubble shadowing his sculpted mouth and stubborn jaw line because he needed to shave twice a day. She felt like a vulture swooping down greedily on every tiny intimate detail of him and her tummy hollowed with a sense of dread, for she had never felt so vulnerable.

Zahir focused on the fluid sway of her hips encased in colourful silk as she moved ahead of him. He guessed she had just stepped out of the shower and was naked beneath those swirling folds of fabric and he was assailed by a slew of highly erotic images that sent a surge of lust shooting straight to his groin. He gritted his even white teeth and flung his arrogant dark head high. He knew what he was doing; he knew exactly what he was doing *this* time. He might have ditched his sense of honour but he had made a decision he could live with. Nobody was perfect, nobody followed every rule… Imperfection had suddenly become newly acceptable to him.

Saffy turned round and regarded him expectantly, her gaze slanting out of a direct meeting with his shrewd eyes and focusing on his wide sensual mouth instead. Instantly she felt hunger flare like a storm in her pelvis and perspiration beaded her short upper lip as she fought the weakness and tried to crush it out. But her body, it seemed, had discovered a treacherous life all of its own and she was suddenly aware of the heaviness of her tender breasts and the straining, aching peaks.

'That five million you told me about?' she prompted with deliberate tartness of tone, keen for him to take his leave again.

'My London lawyer set up the fund with your solicitor. But five years ago nobody involved was aware that your solicitor was in the early stages of senile dementia and, sadly, he didn't do his job properly,' Zahir explained grimly. 'You were not informed about the fund as you should have been and when your solicitor took early retirement through ill health, his son took over his legal practice. When the son realised that you were ignorant of the money accumulating every month, he committed fraud.'

'*Fraud?*' Saffy parroted, her bright blue eyes widening.

'He's been syphoning off the funds for his own benefit ever since. I have put the matter in the hands of the police,' Zahir informed her grimly. 'I owe you an apology for accusing you of having excessively enriched yourself since our divorce.'

Saffy lifted her chin. 'Yes, you do.'

'In spite of everything, I did intend for you to have that money as security and I am very angry that you did not receive it,' he admitted shortly. 'It is possible that you would never have become a model had you known that you were already financially secure.'

Saffy blinked in surprise at that suggestion. 'I doubt that. Had I known about the fund, I would have refused to accept it. We were married for such a short time that I didn't feel that you owed me anything.'

'You were my wife and my responsibility. I felt differently,' Zahir disagreed with unblemished cool.

'If you'd still had a large financial stake in my future, I wouldn't have felt free to put our marriage behind me,' Saffy admitted with quiet dignity as she began moving back to the door with obvious intent. 'But since I didn't know about the fund, it hardly matters now. I'm just relieved you've managed to sort it out. Now, if that's all you have to say—'

'No, it's not all. I have something else I wish to discuss.'

Saffy froze in her tracks and slowly turned back to him. 'If it's anything to do with the recent past, it's unwelcome and I don't want to hear it.'

Zahir regarded her with glittering dark golden eyes. 'Tough,' he told her. 'I'm here and you'll listen.'

'Look, that kind of attitude may go down well in Maraban but it leaves me cold!'

'But I don't…leave you cold,' he affixed as if she might be in some doubt as to his meaning.

A flush of pink washed from her long slender throat up in a wave of burning mortification, for to have him throw that in her face was an affront of no mean order. 'I'm not listening, Zahir… I'm going to show you out. I want you to leave.'

Instead he stalked towards her like a prowling jungle cat cornering a prey. 'No, you don't. You're being stubborn. You don't like the tables being turned but you put this ball into my court—'

'No, I didn't!' Saffy exclaimed in angry vexation.

'You came to me willingly—'

'I said I wasn't going to talk about this!' Saffy flung back at him furiously.

Zahir sent the door behind her crashing shut with an imperious shove of one strong hand. 'I have a proposition I want you to consider—'

'No…*no*.' Saffy whipped up her hands to press them against her ears in desperate defiance. 'I'm not listening. You've got nothing to say that I could want to hear.'

Zahir grabbed her hands and yanked them down, retaining a firm hold on her wrists. 'I've already bought you an apartment here in London. You'll move out of this one into it and I will visit you there whenever I am free…'

As simple shock winged through Saffy in a tidal wave her hands went limp in his grasp and she stared up at him wide-eyed with astonishment and no small amount of incredulity. 'An apartment? What on earth are you suggesting?'

'That you leave your current lover and become mine,' Zahir spelt out with barely leashed ferocity. 'I don't want you here with him. I don't care what arrangement you have. I will only come to you if you are mine alone!'

Saffy blinked rapidly, processing his words in disbelief. 'You're insane. Five years ago, you divorced me and cast me off like an old shoe you'd outgrown!' she condemned rawly. 'And now you're asking me to be your mistress?'

Brilliant dark eyes narrowed and he freed her hands. 'That's an emotive label and rather outdated.'

'And yet you've got the nerve to suggest such a demeaning relationship might suit me?' Saffy hissed at him furiously.

'Yes, I have the nerve,' Zahir declared in a driven undertone, his accent very thick. 'I want you to the edge of madness but I won't share you with other men.'

'My goodness,' Saffy said in a sharp and brittle voice. 'Was I that good in the tent?'

'Stop it,' Zahir urged harshly, stroking a stern finger across her parted lips, leaving a tingle in the wake of his warning. 'Don't reduce us both to that level with that tongue of yours. There is no sin in us indulging ourselves in pleasure. Who would it harm? We would be discreet. I would spend as much time with you as I can find to spare.'

But Saffy was still stunned by what he was proposing. A mistress? A kept woman in the background of his life, a *dirty* secret? *Her?* He had to be kidding. Her pride and independence would never allow her to accept such a relationship. Of course, how could he know that? At eighteen she had been loving, clingy and needy and that was probably how he still saw her. Back then marriage and a man she loved had been the zenith of her ambitions. But the more she thought of it the insult of what he was prepared to offer her in the present cut very deep indeed and she could not credit that he would believe even for a second that she could agree to be any man's secret mistress!

'It really is time that you go,' Saffy snapped, throwing her head back, damp golden hair rippling back from her taut cheekbones. 'You've said what you wanted to say and my answer is no. No, no, *no!* I like my life just the way it is.'

'Look at me and tell me you don't want me,' Zahir growled.

And she looked and lingered on those lean, darkly handsome features and lost, blue eyes fearlessly clashing with smouldering gold, and then it was as if a knot were unfurling faster and faster inside her, unleashing a disturbing blast of emotions and responses that shook her inside out. But even then in the midst of that gathering storm she knew that no way would she ever sink low enough to become his mistress. Yes, she wanted him, but no, she would never take what he was offering because the price was too high.

Saffy parted her lips. 'I don't want you enough for that…'

Zahir glowered down at her. 'Liar.'

Saffy tossed her head. 'You can't bully me into giving you the answer you want—'

'I don't bully you. I have never bullied you,' Zahir countered wrathfully.

'You've very domineering.'

'You like it,' he told her with a roughened edge to his voice, lush black lashes low over his gaze as he watched the tip of her tongue snake out to moisten her lower lip.

'I like my men civilised,' Saffy shot back scornfully.

'But you still want me,' Zahir framed with hungry intensity.

'As I said…not enough to become your personal, private slut,' she spelt out succinctly, but her breathing pattern was fracturing, her tension so great as he came closer that it was like a tightening band constraining her lungs.

'Prove it,' he said, backing her up against the wall, winding long brown fingers into her golden hair to anchor her in place, and drew her head up.

Saffy trembled, pink flying into her cheeks. 'No kissing, no anything,' she warned him. 'I won't let you do this to me—'

And being Zahir, who had a lot in common with an express train when he was set on a goal, he simply ignored her, bending his head, nuzzling her throat, licking a delicate path along her collarbone with such erotic skill that the pulse there went crazy. Her hands knotted into fists at her side to prevent herself from touching him even while the lips he had so far ignored tingled and burned for attention.

'And how dare you offer me *that* option?' Saffy continued heatedly, her rancour on that point unforgotten.

'He who does not dare *loses*,' Zahir traded with assurance, welding his hard, demanding mouth to hers in an explosion of passion that sent her heart racing and the blood pumping insanely fast through her veins.

'What the heck are you playing at?' she gasped strickenly, appalled by the insidious weakness spreading through her lower limbs and the glow of heat and yearning firing up low in her pelvis.

'I'm not playing,' Zahir said thickly, returning to plunder her mouth, sliding his tongue in and out between her parted lips and then delving deep in a sensual assault that made tiny shudders rack her tall, shapely frame. He pressed her back against the wall and even through the barrier of the suit she could feel him hard and urgent and ready. 'I want you. I have wanted you every day since you left Maraban… I can't sleep for wanting you!'

And although words were easy to say and often empty, something still quickened and tightened inside Saffy's chest when he admitted that she exerted that much influence over him. Her robe came undone as he jerked it loose, sliding a hand below it to trail his fingers up her inner thigh. Instantly every sense went on red alert. In that moment she wanted him to touch her more than she had ever wanted anything and she went rigid with anticipation, unable to breathe for longing.

She burned; she *ached*. And then with one stroke of his clever fingers he found her and an agonised moan was wrenched from her as he toyed with her tender flesh, rubbing the tiny bud that controlled her until she strained against him, whimpering, quivering, helpless with need while he explored the slick, hot heat between her legs and she gasped under his marauding mouth. Time had no meaning for her. Indeed it felt as if the world had speeded up because she was so frantically impatient, every skin cell reaching for the climax her body was so desperate to experience.

Zahir paused and she heard the sound of a zip, the crackle of foil and she blinked like someone coming out of the dark into the light, but her hunger didn't abate even a little when she met stunning coal-black-fringed golden eyes alight with desire. She trembled, tried to reason and discovered that she was quite incapable of logic in the grip of the uncontrollable need clawing at her like a kind of madness…terrifying and overwhelming, utterly shameless in its single-minded focus.

'I cannot take you to another man's bed,' Zahir growled, snaking one arm round her waist to lift her off her feet. 'Wrap your legs round me,' he urged.

And she did, hungry for him to put his mouth back on hers, unbearably hungry for him to touch her again. Her arms locked round his neck to steady herself and he braced her against the wall while he angled his hips and lowered her until she felt the smooth, hot crown of his bold shaft pushing against her most tender flesh. Her eyes widened to their fullest, her head rolling back on her shoulders as he slowly, strongly pressed his passage up into her tight sheath. Her excitement went into a tail-spin as he stretched her with his fullness, his grunt of all-male satisfaction vibrating sexily in her ear. He angled her back, withdrew from her achingly tender flesh and then brought her down again hard, sending shock-waves of sensation pounding through her lower body.

'You're so tight,' he growled through gritted teeth, repeating the movement until he was fully seated inside her. 'You feel *so* good. I would kill for this!'

'Don't stop!' she cried, shivering as another wild, exhilarating wave of pleasure-pain pulsed through her pelvis, pushing the excitement higher until it was all-consuming and she was battered by both frustration and uncontrollable need.

'I *couldn't...*' Zahir husked, positioning his hips, grinding against her and withdrawing before driving home again hard. Over and over he repeated that movement until she was literally roused to screaming point.

And the first throbbing upsurge of climax splintered through her like a lightning bolt then and she cried out as the successive spasms of intense pleasure rippled through her. He came with a shudder and a shout and slowly, gently, lowered her legs back down to the floor, which was unfortunate because her legs didn't want to hold her up. She tipped forward as he balanced her, hands strong on her slim shoulders, and he kissed her breathless in the interim before lifting his tousled dark head and saying with typical practicality, 'Where's the bathroom?'

She told him and had to stagger back against the wall to stay upright. She was feeling horribly dizzy. Shock was tearing through her every bit as powerfully as the orgasm had. He had had her against the wall and it had been hideously, horribly thrilling but she didn't want to accept that she had not only let that happen but urged him on to commit that sin. Her knees wanted to give way but she wouldn't let them. With shaking hands, she tied the sash on her robe and covered herself up. A little late, a snide voice remarked in her brain and she squashed it. Her body was still pulsing from his possession and she was weak as water, drained by disbelief at what she had allowed to take place between them.

'Are you OK?' Zahir asked huskily from the doorway.

Saffy shot him a look from below her tumbled hair that would have slaughtered a weaker man where he stood. 'Not really,' she answered truthfully.

'You're very pale—perhaps you should sit down.'

Saffy dropped down onto the nearest sofa, lowered her head and breathed in slow and deep while she fought to reclaim her composure. Her head was swimming, her skin damp with perspiration and she felt slightly sick.

'When would you like to move out?' Zahir enquired smoothly. 'Give me a date and I will have all the arrangements made for you. There will be no hassle, no inconvenience—'

'*Move out?*' Saffy questioned blankly. 'I'm not moving anywhere!'

'You can't continue to live here with McDonald.'

With unsteady hands Saffy caught up her trailing hair and shoved it back from her clammy face as she clumsily sat up. 'What just happened was a bad idea. A *really* bad idea and letting you keep me in an apartment somewhere as a mistress is never going to happen, Zahir. Just accept that.'

'I will not accept it.'

Saffy sprang up on a surge of temper and just as suddenly the room seemed to spin violently around her. Disorientated, she swayed sickly, so dizzy she couldn't focus and she couldn't combat the rising tide of darkness that engulfed her as she fainted.

With a sharp imprecation, Zahir snatched her limp body up from the wooden floor and he settled her down on the sofa. Saffy recovered consciousness quickly and blinked in confusion to find him on his knees beside her. 'What happened?'

'You just dropped where you stood,' Zahir breathed tautly. 'Did I hurt you? Are you ill?'

Her lashes fluttered in bemusement as she dimly registered the sound of the front door slamming. 'No,' she whispered weakly. 'But I think the real problem may be that I'm pregnant...'

'Pregnant?' Zahir exclaimed, his strong bone structure pulling taut below his olive skin. 'When did you get pregnant?'

'Oh, dear,' a familiar voice interposed from the door, which Zahir had left ajar. 'Is this one of those moments when I walk out and come back in making more noise so that you know that I'm here?'

'Cameron?' Saffy craned her neck and began to sit up as her flatmate stared at her anxiously from across the room. Her brain felt as lively as sludge. She had not meant to blurt out her suspicion that she might be pregnant; she had simply spoken her thoughts out loud and now felt exceedingly foolish. 'I fainted. I've never done that in my life before.'

'There's a first time for everything,' Cameron said soothingly.

'Pregnant,' Zahir said again as though he could not get past that single word, and he studied Cameron grimly. '*Your* child?'

'No, you can leave me out of this little chat. I bat for the other team,' Cameron confided with a wry smile. 'You need to make an urgent appointment with the doctor, Saffy.'

Zahir's brow indented. 'What do you mean?' he queried.

'I'm her gay best friend and you can only be Zahir,' Cameron responded ruefully. 'The guards at the front door and the limo flying the little flag parked outside are a dead giveaway.'

'You're gay?' Zahir murmured wrathfully, and he fixed brilliant dark golden eyes accusingly on Saffy. 'Why didn't you tell me that?'

'It was none of your business.'

'And the baby?' Zahir prompted tautly.

'Excuse me,' Cameron said quietly, and he walked back out of the room, carefully closing the door in his wake.

Sitting up then because she no longer felt light-headed, Saffy swung her feet down onto the floor and swivelled round to face Zahir. 'Look, I don't even know yet if I am pregnant,' she admitted heavily. 'I have a test but I haven't used it yet. My suspicions may just be my imagination.'

His face granite hard, Zahir studied her intently like a male struggling to concentrate on only one thing at a time. 'If he's gay, why do you live with him?'

'Because he's my friend and we both were keen to buy an apartment at the same time. We get on very well,' Saffy told him wryly, wishing she had bitten her tongue out of her head before letting drop the fact that she suspected that she might be pregnant, for such a threat—and she had no doubt that he would see it as a threat—would only create more stormy waves in her dealings with Zahir.

'If McDonald's gay, why do people believe you and he are a couple?' Zahir persisted.

Saffy sighed. 'Cameron was raised by elderly grand-parents and he's very attached to them. He doesn't think they could accept his sexuality and he says he won't come out of the closet until they're gone.'

'So, in the meantime he uses you for cover.'

'We use each other,' Saffy parried without hesitation. 'I get bothered less by aggressive men as long as Cameron appears to be part of my life. Now can we please leave my friend out of this discussion?'

Zahir gritted his even white teeth together. 'Pregnant,' he repeated afresh.

'Maybe, maybe not,' Saffy muttered wearily. 'Look, I'll go and do the wretched test now and we'll see if there's anything to worry about.'

'If it is true, how will we know whether or not it is mine?' Zahir demanded icily.

'Don't make me slap you, Zahir. I haven't the energy right now,' Saffy sighed unhappily, moving past him.

Long brown fingers snapped round her wrist to hold her still. 'Do you have any idea how major an event this could be for a man in my position?' he raked down at her.

'No and, right now, I don't want to think about it. I only want to find out if there is anything for us to worry about. You shouldn't have come here, Zahir. You should have kept your distance. What happened between us in Maraban ended there. You're screwing up my life,' Saffy condemned, dragging her arm angrily free.

'It won't be at an end if you're carrying my child.'

Without another word, Saffy trudged through the hall to the bathroom, retrieved the test kit from the cupboard and pulled out the instructions. Minutes later she stood at the window holding the wand, waiting to see the result. She still felt shell-shocked by the explosive passion that had erupted between them, had never dreamt that she could lose control of her own body to such an extent, had not even suspected that the desire for sex might so badly betray her principles. Of course it had not occurred to her either that she would see him again, that he would deliberately seek her out in London or tell her that he couldn't sleep for *wanting* her. At least she wasn't the only one of them tossing and turning sleepless in the dark of the night, she thought wretchedly. But without the smallest warning, everything had changed. She had believed she could shrug off their encounter in Maraban; she had tried to tell herself that she had used him. In short, she reflected painfully, she had told herself a whole lot of face-saving rubbish in an effort to persuade herself that she was fully in control of events and now reality was banging very loudly at her door.

Almost absent-mindedly she looked down at the wand in her hand and her entire body froze. She gulped in a breath, checked her watch, gazed down transfixed at the line that had formed just as the instructions had explained. Her legs suddenly felt so woolly she had to perch on the side of the bath. *Be careful of what you wish for...*for according to the test result, she was pregnant. For a split second a rush of joy consumed her and then she recalled Zahir's hard, forbidding expression and she groaned out loud, for nothing but complications lay ahead. Zahir and an accidental pregnancy would be a very dangerous combination: Zahir liked to plan everything; Zahir had to be in control; Zahir had been raised in a culture in which such a development was totally unacceptable, socially, morally and every other way there was.

Why, oh, why had she opened her silly mouth and told him? Regret touched her deep. Now whether she liked it or not he was involved and it would have been much better for both of them if he was not. She didn't want him involved. Even less did she want him to be hostile to her condition. She might never before have allowed herself to dream of having a baby, but she would never, ever have chosen to have a child by a man who couldn't possibly want either of them.

Saffy walked back into the living room where Zahir was drinking coffee—Cameron evidently having played host in her absence—and staring moodily out of the window. He didn't like cities: he felt claustrophobic in them. Why did she still remember that? Hearing her entrance, he swung round, stunning dark golden eyes shooting straight to her pale, tight features.

And he knew, that fast he knew, read the defensiveness there and the reluctance to get any closer to him. Why? Was she afraid of him now? Did she think that in some way he meant her harm? Her golden hair had dried into loose, undisciplined waves round her lovely oval face and her eyes were incredibly blue against her pallor. Even with strain etched in every line of her visage she was hauntingly beautiful.

'We do have something to worry about,' she confirmed.

Zahir released his breath in a slow hiss, not a muscle moving on his lean bronzed face. 'I thought you were taking the contraceptive pill.'

'You assumed I was. I saw no reason to tell you otherwise because I didn't think this situation would arise,' Saffy admitted doggedly, determined to be honest now because matters had become too serious for her to risk even half-truths.

'Why were you not taking precautions to protect yourself against this development?' he demanded.

'I had no reason to. I wasn't having sex with anyone, so you don't need to wonder whose child it is,' she told him tightly, colour mantling her cheekbones.

'Naturally I will wonder. I have no wish to offend you but I was certainly under the impression that you had other lovers,' Zahir countered flatly.

'Don't believe all that you read in the papers,' Saffy advised, lifting her head high, her blue eyes guarded.

'I don't but, even allowing for a fair amount of exaggeration and invented stories, there is room for me to doubt the likelihood that in one brief encounter I have fathered your child,' Zahir fielded very quietly.

'I didn't think it was very likely either, but we're both young and healthy, it was the wrong time of the month for me to have an accident and clearly you have killer sperm,' Saffy told him drily.

'Don't make a joke of it,' Zahir growled.

'I can't prove it's your baby until after it's born,' Saffy murmured ruefully. 'DNA testing is too risky during pregnancy. On the other hand you could think back sensibly to that day in the tent and appreciate that ironically you are the only lover I've *ever* had.'

Zahir frowned, winged ebony brows pleating above questioning dark as night eyes flaring with disbelief. 'That is not possible.'

'Forget the newspaper stories and your prejudices and think about it rationally,' Saffy urged with quiet dignity, determined not to allow him to continue to cherish doubts about who had fathered her child. 'You're not stupid—I know you're not. I was a virgin.'

All colour bled from below his olive-toned complexion as he stared back at her with smouldering golden force and she recognised the exact moment when he recalled the blood stains on the bed because he suddenly swore in Arabic, tore his stunned gaze from hers and half swung away from her, his lean brown hands clenching into fists. 'If that is true, I have greatly wronged you,' he bit out rawly.

'We wronged each other a long time ago,' Saffy cut in. 'I *chose* to share that bed with you. It was my decision and this is my…er, problem.'

'If it's my child, it's mine too and I don't see our child as a problem,' Zahir retorted with a harsh edge to his dark deep voice. 'We'll remarry just as soon as I can arrange it.'

'Remarry?' Saffy gasped in wonderment. 'You have to be joking!'

'Our child's future is too serious to joke about and it can only be secured through marriage.'

'And we all know how that turned out the last time,' Saffy returned doggedly, fighting to think logically because his proposal had shaken her to her very depths. Was he serious? Was he really serious?

'When my father died and I took the throne, everything changed in Maraban,' Zahir declared levelly. 'We would be able to lead normal lives now. You're pregnant. Of course, I want to marry you.'

Saffy was reeling from a dozen different reactions:

disbelief, scorn, anger, frustration among them. Zahir was set on taking charge as usual. He wasn't reacting on a personal level, he was reacting as a public figure, keen to hide an embarrassing mistake within the respectability of marriage.

'I don't want to marry you just because I'm pregnant.'

'And what do you think your child would want?' Zahir shot that icily controlled demand back at her. 'If you don't marry me, you will deprive that child of a father and of the status in life he or she has a right to enjoy. Without marriage, the child will have to remain secret and it will be almost impossible for me to establish a normal relationship with him or her.'

In one cool statement, Zahir had given Saffy a lot to think about, but then faster than the speed of light her child had gone from being a line on a test wand to a living, breathing being, who might well question her decisions at a later date. For the first time she appreciated that she could not continue to put her own wants and needs first because, whatever she chose to do, she would, one day, have to take responsibility for the choices she had made on her child's behalf.

'We could get married just to ensure that the baby was legitimate…and then get another divorce,' she suggested tautly.

Brilliant dark eyes flamed golden as flames. 'Is that really the very best you can offer? Is the prospect of being my wife again such a sacrifice?'

Saffy studied the floor. She thought of the wicked forbidden delight of his passion, recognising that on that level everything between them had radically changed. She looked up, feeling the instant mesmeric pull of him the moment she saw his lean dark face. Her heart hammered inside her, her mouth running dry.

'Couldn't you give our marriage a second chance?' Zahir asked huskily.

'It's too soon to consider that,' Saffy argued. 'The first thing I need to do now is see my doctor and confirm that I *am* pregnant. Then we'll decide what to do. Look at this from my point of view. When you arrived here, you asked me to be your mistress…now suddenly you're talking marriage, but I don't want to get married purely because you accidentally got me pregnant.'

Zahir surveyed her with stormy intensity and the atmosphere thickened as though laced with cracked ice. 'I believe in fate, not accidents. What is meant to be will be.'

Saffy rolled her eyes, compressed her lips and stood up. 'You shipped me out to the desert for seduction, not fatherhood. You brought this roof down over our ears—you sort it out!'

'Marriage will sort it out,' he contended stubbornly.

'Oh, if only it were that simple.'

'But it is.' Before she could even guess his intention, he had closed a hand over hers. His brilliant gaze sought and held hers by sheer force of will. 'Right now, it's the best choice you can make. Let go of the past. Trust me to look after you and my child. I will not let you down.'

'And would you agree to a divorce at a later date?'

Saffy prompted shakily, more impressed than she wanted to be by his promise of good intentions.

'If that's what you wanted, if you were unhappy as you were before, yes,' Zahir agreed grittily, not choosing to add the unpleasant realities that would accompany any such decision on her part. Complete honesty was not possible. What really mattered was getting that ring back on her finger and securing their child's future. 'This is not about us, this is about our child, what he or she needs most.'

'If you really mean that…' Saffy drew in a ragged breath, terrified of the confusing thoughts teeming through her head. She was trying very hard to put the welfare of her child first and not muddy the waters with the bitterness of the past and the insecurity of the present. He would keep his promise: she knew that. On that level she trusted him and she quite understood that he wanted their child to have the very best start in life possible. They owed their child that chance.

'I do,' Zahir confirmed levelly.

'Then on that basis, I agree.' So great was the stress of making that announcement that Saffy felt light-headed again as all the little devils in her memory banks began queuing up to remind her of how vulnerable she would be if she put herself in Zahir's power again.

Zahir released her hand. 'I'll organise it.'

He got as far as the door before Saffy called him back to say tautly, 'I want a *proper* wedding.'

'Meaning?' Zahir sought to clarify.

'No hole-in-the-corner do in the embassy for me this

time,' Saffy spelled out with scorn. 'I want a bridal
gown and a family occasion with my sisters as brides-
maids and all the rest of the wedding hoopla.'

Taken aback by the admission, Zahir literally paled.

'Those are my terms and I won't budge on them,'
Saffy completed doggedly.

CHAPTER SEVEN

'ARE YOU REALLY sure about doing this?' Kat looked tense and anxious and Saffy immediately felt guilty.

What had she been thinking of when she dragged her family into all of this? A shotgun wedding, no less. Her sister, Kat, didn't need the stress but she had insisted on organising the wedding within the space of one incredibly short week and had proven that if sufficient money was thrown at a challenge, it could be done. Saffy studied her reflection in the mirror. Her gorgeous designer wedding dress was a classic, nipped in at the waist for shape and falling in fluid folds to her satin-clad feet. She wasn't wearing a veil: the hairdresser had piled her hair up and topped it with the magnificent sapphire and diamond tiara Zahir had sent to her. Matching drop earrings sparkled with every movement she made.

'Saffy?' the attractive redhead pressed. 'You know, it may be your wedding day but it's still not too late to change your mind. You don't *have* to marry Zahir. You don't have to do this to please anybody.'

Looking reflective, Saffy breathed in deep. 'I really do want to give our baby the chance to have two par-

ents. None of us ever had that. My sisters and I had you
and you were a brilliant stand-in Mum,' she told Kat
warmly. 'But I'd like to try it the old-fashioned way before I try to go it alone.'

Kat frowned. 'You're not in a very optimistic mood
for a new bride.'

'I'm being realistic. Zahir will commit to being a
father—I know that about him and I respect him for
it. If marriage works for us, it works, and if it doesn't
work, at least I'll have tried,' Saffy muttered ruefully.

'I just can't believe you got involved with him again.
It's like fatal attraction without the bunny boiler. I
mean, five years ago Zahir broke your heart and I don't
want him doing it again.' Her sister sighed unhappily.
'Mikhail has checked him out and he says Maraban is
stable now and that Zahir seems to be one of the good
guys.'

'I could've told you that,' Saffy interrupted heatedly.

'And there's no sleazy stories about him either,' Kat
added in a suitably quiet undertone. 'Obviously there's
been women but not in the kind of numbers you need
to worry about.'

Saffy ground her teeth together in silence, wishing
that her Russian billionaire brother-in-law had minded
his own business when it came to Zahir. Even as she
thought it she knew she was wronging the man. Undoubtedly Kat's concerns about her sister's bridegroom
had prompted Mikhail's investigation into Zahir's reputation. 'He would never be sleazy,' Saffy declared,

suppressing her recollection of that invitation to be his mistress.

'Are you upset about Emmie refusing to come today?' Kat asked ruefully.

'No.' Saffy lied sooner than add additional worry to Kat's caring heart. 'I can understand her not wanting to get into a bridesmaid's frock when she's so pregnant and I can also understand her saying that she's not in the mood.'

'Some day soon, you two need to sit down and talk and sort out the aggro between you.'

'Easier said than done with Emmie always avoiding me like the plague,' Saffy countered ruefully. 'I phoned her and said I understood her not wanting to be a bridesmaid but would love her to come just as a guest and she said she wasn't feeling well enough to travel.'

'Well, she has had a pretty tough time being pregnant, so that probably wasn't a lie,' Kat conceded. 'It makes me wonder if I'm wise to be considering IVF in case that kind of sickness and nausea in pregnancy runs in the family.'

'I'm not feeling sick…not yet, anyway,' Saffy pointed out bracingly, smiling as Topsy bounced into the room, bubbling with excitement in her glittering green bridesmaid's dress and quite unaware of the serious chat her older sisters had been involved in. It seemed natural to the three sisters that neither Saffy's mother nor her father were taking part in the coming ceremony. Saffy had had virtually nothing to do with her mother, Odette, or her father since they had abandoned her to foster care when she was twelve years old. Her parents had divorced when she was much younger and the bitterness of their estrangement had had an inevitable effect on her father's attitude to his twin daughters. He had left them behind and moved on. Although Kat had encouraged Saffy to foster a forgiving attitude towards their mother, Saffy had too many memories of childhood neglect to do so. Odette simply wasn't a loving parent and never had been.

The wedding took place at the church only a few doors down from Kat and Mikhail's London home. The church's rather gloomy interior had been transformed with an abundance of white and pink flowers and knotted ribbons. Saffy walked down the aisle on Cameron's arm, her heart banging like a drum at a rock concert when she finally got close enough to see Zahir's imperious dark head at the altar. How did he feel about this? How did he *really* feel? Throughout the past crazy busy week while she packed up her life in London her only contact with Zahir had been by phone. She had rung him after the doctor had confirmed her pregnancy. He had rung her several times to find out about the wedding schedule. There had been nothing intimate about those exchanges.

She had also ploughed through a half-dozen frustrating meetings with her agent and various clients as the reality of her condition forced the need for urgent rethinks on previously planned shoots. A couple of clients had taken the opportunity to drop her because her pregnancy meant that she was in breach of contract.

Desert Ice, however, had retained her services because they were more than halfway through their campaign. She was grateful for that because it was mainly her earnings from the cosmetics company that funded the orphanage she supported.

Zahir's stunning black-fringed golden eyes met hers as she drew level with him and she felt painfully vulnerable, which she didn't like at all. Unfortunately wounding memories of their first wedding were assailing her, reminding her of a day when she had not had a doubt in the world about becoming a wife, had indeed innocently overflowed with feelings of love and happiness. The wedding ring slid onto her finger and she breathed in deep, conscious that Zahir retained a hold on her hand. It was done, the die was cast, she told herself soothingly. What was she afraid of happening? What was there to fear now? That he didn't love her—well, she knew he didn't love her, didn't she? Unfortunately the awareness that he was marrying her to give their baby a name and a home was no more welcome to her heart or her pride.

On their passage back down the aisle, Zahir pressed a supportive hand to her spine. 'You feel very shaky,' he admitted when she cast him an enquiring glance.

And it was true, she did feel shaky, had ridden roughshod over her misgivings to marry him, trying at every step to put her child's needs ahead of her own.

Zahir participated in the photographs in silence. Sapphire was pale as death and silent and her family, aside of the little bouncy one in green, who had smiled brightly at him, were clearly hostile and suspicious. No doubt her family had taken their cues from Sapphire. She didn't want to be married to him again; he could feel it in the tension that gripped her every time he touched her. That made him angry and bitter, roused memories better left buried. But he had royally screwed up by allowing his primal instincts to triumph and there was always a price to be paid for recklessness, he reminded himself darkly. He had got her back. That was, at least, a beginning, and only time would tell whether or not she would continue to hold the threat of a divorce like a gun to his head.

'You look stunning,' Zahir told her belatedly as she scrambled into the limo that would whisk them from the church to the embassy to undergo a Muslim marriage ceremony. 'How are you feeling?'

'I'm not ill, only pregnant,' Saffy countered defensively, wishing he hadn't reminded her of her condition, reluctant to be viewed as in any way in need of special treatment.

The second ceremony was brief, witnessed by embassy officials and a posed photograph was taken afterwards. They returned to Mikhail and Kat's house where a reception was being held in the ballroom. After the wedding breakfast, they circulated. Surrounded by the familiar faces of the models she often worked with, Saffy began to relax a little, bearing up well to comments about how quiet she had been about her supposed long-term relationship with Zahir and striving to behave more like a normal bride.

'Of course, I shouldn't mention it,' trilled Natasha,

a six-foot-tall Ukrainian blonde, well on her way to supermodel status. 'But Zahir was mine first.'

It was said so quietly and with such a sunny smile that it took several seconds for that spiteful confession to sink in on Saffy. She stared back into Natasha's very pale blue eyes and murmured, 'Really?' as politely as if the other woman had commented on the weather.

'Yes, a couple of years ago now. A fling at a film festival,' Natasha confided with a little shrug of a designer-clad shoulder. 'But he was hard to forget.'

'Yes,' Saffy acknowledged, passing on as soon as she could into less aggressive company, anger licking like fire at her composure. Mine first? No, he had been hers, her husband and then her ex-husband before he became anyone else's. But the truth that he had sought amusement in other beds could still slash like a knife turning in her breast. She glanced back at Natasha, beautiful and reputedly sexually voracious, struggling not to picture Zahir entwined in her arms, and the nausea she had never experienced until that moment turned her stomach into a washing machine and sent sickness hurtling up her throat. Her skin clammy with perspiration, she rushed off to the cloakroom and made it just in time. She was horribly sick and it took a few minutes for her to freshen up and lose the unsteadiness that afflicted her in the aftermath.

When she emerged, Topsy was waiting for her. 'Are you OK? Zahir saw you leaving and asked me to check.'

Zahir didn't miss much, Saffy reflected wretchedly.

'I think I just got bitten by morning sickness.' And a very tall shrewish blonde.

But Saffy was no fan of ducking reality and she knew she had to deal with life as it was. Zahir had been with other women when he was no longer married to her and that was his business, not hers. His past was his own, just as hers would have been had she lived a little more dangerously since their first marriage. But unfortunately there had not been a cure for the fact that she had still found Zahir and her memory of him far more attractive than other men. What did that say about her? He was like a habit she had never managed to shake, her one and only fantasy, and the men who had pursued her over the years had never managed to cause her a single sleepless night. With the exception of Zahir, she had never pined for a phone call or a smile from a man, had truly never contrived to rouse that much interest, and perhaps that was why she had fallen so easily back into bed with him. Was it a kind of persistent physical infatuation? Had he somehow spoiled her for other men? She stared at him as she crossed the floor of the ballroom.

He was lithe, powerfully built and supremely sophisticated in his light grey morning suit with his luxuriant ebony hair fanning back from his brow; his dark deepset eyes were riveting in his lean, bronzed face. He was drop-dead gorgeous and always had been a very hard act to follow. But as her body stirred with responses far removed from nausea, her breasts swelling and peaking beneath her bodice and a dull ache expanding in her pelvis, she was furious with herself for being so susceptible to a male who neither loved nor even truly wanted her.

'What's wrong?' Zahir asked softly.

'Why would anything be wrong?' she traded tartly, ice in her cool scrutiny and edging her voice. 'You tell me…film festival two years ago, Ukrainian blonde by the name of Natasha, ring any bells?' That scornful and provocative question just leapt off Saffy's tongue before she was even aware she was going to voice it.

The faintest hint of colour edged Zahir's chiselled cheekbones but his dark golden gaze did not waver from hers. Indeed if anything he stood a little straighter. 'I will never lie to you.'

Even when you should, she almost screamed at him, wanting, needing to know and yet fearing what knowing more would do to her.

'There weren't many and there was nothing serious,' Zahir breathed in a harsh undertone. 'This is not a conversation I want to have on our wedding day.'

'It's not something I want to talk about either!' Saffy launched back at him, her eyes a very bright blue lit with anger.

His stubborn jaw line squared. 'Before you judge me, ask yourself if you have any idea of what state I was in after our divorce.'

Saffy came over all defensive. 'How would I know?'

'When you're ready to tell me what changed you out of all recognition in the bedroom, I'll tell you why I did what I did.' His brilliant dark eyes glittered. It was a challenge, blunt and simple, and it only made Saffy angrier than ever.

He had divorced her. *He* had made that choice. He could not expect her to accept the consequences or feel responsible for a situation that had not been of her making. As for what had changed her into a normal sexually able woman, that was not something she was willing to share with him. It was too private, too personal, might well affect the way he looked at her and that very possible outcome made her cringe.

'Are you two actually arguing?' Kat came up to demand in dismay.

'We always did have a fiery relationship,' Zahir admitted.

'Not so different from our own,' Kat's husband, Mikhail, teased his wife. 'It takes time to adjust to living with another person.'

'Time and buckets of patience,' Zahir added, an authoritative look stamped on his lean dark face that only made Saffy want to slap him hard.

'Your guests are waiting for the bride and groom to start the dancing,' Kat informed them more cheerfully.

Saffy wasn't in the mood to dance, especially not with Natasha smirking at the side of the floor, but she owed her sister too much to risk upsetting her and she gave way with good grace.

Zahir was a great dancer with a natural sense of rhythm but Saffy felt as if someone had welded an iron bar to her spine and she was stiff in the circle of his arms, holding herself at a distance. Glimpses of Natasha watching them did not improve her mood. Yes, she had known he had made love to other women, but actually having a face to pin to one of those anonymous women was another turn of the torture screw. She had never thought of herself as the jealous type and now she was finding out different. Once Zahir had been hers, entirely hers, and even though things had gone wrong in the bedroom she had rather naively trusted him not to stray. Now she was wondering crazy things, such as how she compared to his other lovers, and she was regretting her lack of experience and her honesty on that score. Yet how could she have lied when her child's paternity hinged on telling the complete truth? That reminder cooled the fizz in her blood, settled her down and made her seek another topic of conversation.

'I thought you might have invited your brother and sister and possibly even Azel to the wedding,' she remarked gingerly.

'One of Hayat's children is in hospital with complications following on from a bout of measles. Akram is standing in for me at an OPEC meeting and my sister-in-law, Azel, no longer lives with us. She remarried last year and now lives in Dubai,' Zahir explained. 'You will meet what remains of my family tomorrow.'

'I'll look forward to it,' Saffy said politely. 'Do they know about the baby?'

'Only my siblings. When we chose to marry in such haste, it made sense to be honest,' Zahir said wryly.

Hot pink burned like a banner across her cheeks at the thought that his strictly raised siblings might assume that she was a total slut for succumbing so quickly and easily to their brother's attractions.

'You know, when you blush, the tip of your nose turns pink as well,' Zahir husked. 'It's cute as hell.'

'You know what happened in the desert...the baby,' Saffy said sharply. 'It's *all* your fault.'

A sizzling, utterly unexpected smile played across Zahir's wide sensual mouth and startled her. 'I know. But out of it I gained a very beautiful wife and we have a baby in our future and I can't find it within my heart to regret anything we did.'

Her eyes prickled and she blinked rapidly, knowing that her acid and pointless comment had not deserved so generous a response. Suddenly her tension gave and she rested her head down on his broad shoulder, drinking in and loving the familiar scent of him—warm clean male laced with an evocative hint of sandalwood. She was momentarily weak with the sheer amount of emotion pumping through her and so confused, still so desperately confused about what she felt, what she truly thought. With every passing moment, her feelings seemed to swing to one side and then violently to the other. So much had happened between them in such a short time frame that she was mentally all over the place.

Saffy was half asleep by the time they left for the airport. She had changed into a very elegant shift dress and jacket almost the same colour as her eyes and let her hair down to flow round her shoulders in a golden mane. Relaxation was infiltrating her for the first time that day.

Drowsily she studied the platinum ring on her finger. They were married again: she couldn't quite believe it.

'I think I'll sleep all the way to Maraban,' Saffy told him apologetically as they boarded the private jet.

'It's been a long day and it is after midnight,' Zahir conceded wryly. 'But first there's something I'd like to tell you.'

Alert to the guarded note in his dark deep drawl, Saffy felt her adrenalin start to pump. The jet took off and drinks were served. She undid her belt, let the stewardess show her into the sleeping compartment where she freshened up, and then she rejoined Zahir, made herself comfortable and sipped her fresh orange juice. 'So?' she prompted quietly, proud of her patience and self-discipline while she wondered what he had to unveil. 'What is it?'

Zahir straightened his broad shoulders and settled hard dark eyes on her without flinching. 'I've bought the Desert Ice cosmetics company.'

CHAPTER EIGHT

SAFFY BLINKED IN astonishment, for of all the many sur-
prises she had thought Zahir might want to disclose
that one staggering confession had not figured. She set
down her glass and stood up, her mind in a bemused
fog. 'You bought the company? But why? Why the heck
would you do that?'

'It *was* a good investment.' Zahir loosed a sardonic
laugh that bluntly dismissed that explanation. 'But I
bought it only for your benefit. I knew the company
had a cast-iron contract with you and I didn't want anyone putting pressure on you while you were pregnant.'

Eyes slowly widening, Saffy stared back at him in
rampant disbelief, while she wondered what strings he
had pulled to learn the contract terms she had been on
with the company. 'I can't believe that you would inter-
fere in my career to that extent!' she admitted in stunned
disbelief, anger steadily gathering below the surface of
that initial reaction. 'Nobody was putting pressure on
me at the meeting I attended with their campaign man-
ager this week.'

Cynicism hardened Zahir's expressive mouth, making him look inexpressibly tough in a way far different from the younger man she remembered. It was a look that was hard, weathered and unapologetic and she refused to be intimidated by it. 'Naturally not. By that time, I was the new owner, so of course there was no pressure. They can film your face as much as they like while you're pregnant but they'll be doing it in Maraban.'

'In...*Maraban?*' Saffy parroted as though he had suggested somewhere as remote as the moon.

'I don't want you forced to travel thousands of miles round the globe now that you're pregnant. It would be too stressful for you.'

'And what would you know about that?' Saffy demanded hotly. 'What do you know about what a pregnant woman needs?'

'I don't want you exhausted,' Zahir asserted grimly. 'I appreciate that the baby is a development that wasn't planned or, indeed, expected, but adjustments have to be made to your working schedule.'

'You're not the boss of me!' Saffy hissed back at him in helpless outrage. 'You know, the one phrase I heard you speak most clearly was, *"I don't want..."* This is about you, your need to clip my wings and control me. Isn't it enough that I married you? What about what I want? What about what I need? This isn't all about you!'

'I'm not trying to control you.' Eyes now smouldering with anger, Zahir gazed back at her, his hard jaw line set at an unyielding angle. 'But the security needs alone that are now required to ensure your safety would be impossible to maintain in some of the exotic locations where you have recently travelled.'

'I don't have security needs!' Saffy flung at him in a bitterly aggrieved tone of fury. 'It's taken me five years to build my career and I didn't get where I am by being difficult!'

Zahir didn't bat a single absurdly long eyelash. He stared steadily back at her, those twin black fringes round his remarkable eyes merely adding to the intensity of his scrutiny. 'As my wife, you have security needs. Just as I could be a target, you could be as well. I will not allow your headstrong spirit to tempt you into taking unnecessary risks. This is not about your career. This is about you accepting that your new status will demand lifestyle changes. You are no longer Sapphire Marshall, you are a queen.'

'I don't want to be a queen!' Saffy sobbed in a passionate rage at the logic he was firing at her. Memories were flooding back to her of long-buried quarrels during which she had raged while Zahir shot down her every argument with murderous logic and practicality. 'You never told me that. I just thought I'd be your wife, your consort, your plus one or whatever you want to call it!'

'The last queen was my mother, who died when my younger brother was born,' Zahir commented grimly. 'It is time you saw sense. You can't have thought you could marry me and ignore who and what I am.'

Saffy was so worked up she wanted to scream. Over the past week she had thought of many, many things, like dresses and wedding breakfasts and guest lists and babies, but not once had she pondered her future status in Maraban. In fact she hadn't wanted to think about Maraban at all because once she had been very unhappy there.

'I didn't think about it,' Saffy muttered in indignation, furious with him, wondering in a rage how on earth he had broken the news about the Desert Ice company and then contrived to roll over his indefensible interference in her career to put her on the defensive with the news that she was apparently a queen. 'I don't want to be a queen. I'm sure I'm not cut out for it. In fact I bet I'm totally unsuitable to be royal.'

'With that attitude you probably will be,' Zahir shot back at her with derision. 'I think you tried harder at eighteen to fit in than you are willing to try now as an adult.'

Saffy's lush mouth dropped open as temper exploded in her like a grenade. 'I was a doormat at eighteen, a total stupid doormat! I wanted to please you. I wanted to please your family. I was so busy trying to be something I'm not—*and* getting no thanks for it! I had no space to be me!'

'Times have changed. Maraban has been transformed and brought into the twenty-first century. But I have changed as well,' Zahir breathed on a taut warning note, his gaze burning gold in its force. 'I will tell you now how things are and I won't keep secrets from you again.'

'*Secrets?*' Saffy shot back at him jaggedly, entrapped by that one word of admission, her nervous tension seizing on it. '*What secrets?*'

'Five years ago, I kept a lot from you in an attempt to protect you. I didn't want to hurt you but this time I will employ no lies and no half-truths. I will tell it like it is…'

Other women, Saffy was thinking in despair, a sharp wounding pain piercing her somewhere in the chest region. What else could he be talking about? When he had found no satisfaction in the marital bedroom he had gone elsewhere. Maybe out to that remote desert palace where his late father had kept his personal harem, *very* discreet. Hey, Saffy, you dummy, a little voice piped up at the back of her mind…maybe he wasn't on army manoeuvres all those times he was gone. Maybe he was off the leash having fun, the kind of fun you couldn't give him then. And what shook Saffy most at that moment was that instead of confronting him on that score and demanding an explanation, she instead wanted to stay silent and withdraw, conserve some dignity, protect herself from painful revelations that she did not at that moment feel strong enough to bear. Every atom of ESP she possessed urged her to leave the past where it belonged.

Saffy lifted her golden head. 'I'm tired. I'm going to bed but thanks for making our wedding night almost as dreadful as the first we had,' she murmured with stinging scorn.

And she saw right then in his lean darkly handsome face that he had forgotten it was their wedding night. And really that said it all, didn't it? She had already travelled from being the object of intense desire to being the pregnant wife, apparently shorn of attraction.

Zahir gritted his teeth and resisted the urge to talk back to her in a similar vein. Had she really thought he would stage their wedding night on a plane when she was exhausted and already under strain from all the challenges of the past weeks? He suffered a hollow sensation of horror even recalling that first catastrophic wedding night, her sickness, fear and distress, his own incomprehension and sense of defeat. She had been too young, far too young and naïve at eighteen, he knew that now. Guilt assailed him as Saffy ducked into the cabin, her lovely face taut and pale awakening memories he would have done anything to avoid. So much for honesty, so much for trying to clear the air, he reflected bitterly.

That last comment of hers had been a low blow, Saffy conceded in shame. It wasn't either of their faults that their first wedding night had been catastrophic and he had been incredibly kind and patient and understanding even though she knew he didn't understand any more than she did then what was wrong with her. Hitting out at him like that had been unjust, a mean retaliation to the reality that Zahir had made her feel small and stupid with his talk of security concerns and queens. She didn't look much like a queen, she thought wretchedly, studying herself with wet pink eyes in the mirror, noting the mascara and eyeliner smudged from tears. She had panicked when he mentioned that because she was so terrified of not meeting his expectations again. Hadn't she *already* done that to him once? She didn't want to let him down or embarrass him but what did she know about being royal? Certainly she had learned absolutely nothing during their last marriage when only the servants knew she existed and she was virtually the invisible woman.

He didn't love her, didn't want her, probably had no faith in her ability to act like a royal wife either, Saffy thought painfully, tears streaming down her cheeks as she forced her convulsed face into a pillow. Why did she care so much about what he thought of her? Why did it hurt so much that she felt she couldn't stand it? And why more than anything in the world did she now want him to come in and put his arms round her to comfort her the way he had once done without even thinking about it? She had married him to give their baby a better start in life. That was the only reason and she didn't know why she was getting so worked up, sobs shuddering through her body like a storm unleashed on her without warning.

I am not in love with him. I am *so* not in love with him, she told herself urgently. That is not why I'm suddenly looking for more from him than he ever promised to deliver. And in that guarded state of mind she finally fell asleep.

The stewardess wakened her with breakfast and the announcement that the plane would be landing in an hour. Noting that she had slept alone in the bed, Saffy lifted her chin, knowing he had spent the night in one of the reclining seats. Why was she wondering whether he had been unfaithful to her when they had last been married? What did it matter? How was that relevant?

The last thing she needed was to get bound up in the problems of a long-dead past. They weren't the same people any more. Showered and elegantly attired in a print dress and a fine cashmere cardigan, she emerged from the sleeping compartment, feeling as brittle as bone china.

Zahir, sheathed in the beige and white pristine desert robes that accentuated his height and undeniably exotic attributes, gave her a smile that was a masterpiece of civility while wishing her good morning. She almost laughed but, once again, their shared past rattled like a skeleton locked in a cupboard: Zahir was superb at plastering over the cracks and pretending nothing had happened and that last night's divisive dispute had not occurred. Time and time again he had done that to her when they were first married when she tried to have serious talks with him and he shrugged them off, changed the subject, refused to be drawn. Stop it, *stop it,* she urged her disobedient brain, determined not to bring those memories of his evasiveness into the present when so much else had altered.

'We had a row,' she reminded him out of pure spite and resentment of his poise.

'I should never tackle a serious conversation after midnight when we're both tired.' His eyes glittered with unexpected raw amusement and the sheer primal attraction of him in that instant sent a flock of butterflies dancing in her tummy and clenched her muscles tight somewhere a great deal more intimate. Pink flushed her cheeks as he sipped at his coffee, the very image of cool control and sophistication. 'Coffee?'

Saffy served herself from the coffee pot on the table and sat down. 'What you said—'

Zahir shifted a fluid brown hand in a silencing motion. 'No, leave it. It was the wrong time and we have all the time in the world now.'

Saffy tried to steel herself to resist the command note in that assurance and then wondered if perhaps he was right. In any case, did she want confessions if what she suspected was true? Did she really want to stir up the past and perhaps damage the future relationship they might have before this marriage even got off the ground? Such patience, such careful concern felt unfamiliar to her in Zahir's presence, for once she had said whatever she liked to him with absolutely no lock on her tongue. And she wanted that freedom back, she recognised dimly, wanted it back almost more than she wanted anything.

'It's not like you to be so quiet.'

'The Queenie bit pulverised me,' she muttered tightly.

'You're more than up to the challenge,' Zahir asserted smoothly. 'You're accustomed to being in the public eye and right now you look…*wonderful*.'

'Do I?' Saffy hated the sound of that question, her gaze welded to his in search of falsehood, fake flattery, the smallest hint of insincerity.

'You always did and still do. And sadly, although it shouldn't matter, such beauty does impress people,'

Zahir murmured ruefully. 'I've never understood why you're not vain.'

'Other people work and train to do much more important and necessary things than I do but I got where I am because of my face and figure, not my brain or my skills,' Saffy pointed out flatly. 'It's not something to boast about.'

'But you're so much more—you always were,' Zahir declared, reaching for her fingers where they curled in discomfiture on the table top and enclosing them in his warm hand. 'And in Maraban, you will be able to show how much more you are capable of.'

'What does that mean?' Saffy prompted, touched by that hand round hers, energised by the conviction with which he spoke.

'That the woman who gives most of her earnings to an orphanage in Africa will have free rein to raise funds for good works in my country. Yes, I found out about that fact, quite accidentally through your crooked solicitor,' Zahir admitted. 'It made me feel very proud of you.'

Saffy tensed and reddened, wary of praise on the score of one of her biggest secrets. 'The children had so little and I wanted to help them. It made my career seem less superficial when I could feel that I had a worthwhile cause to work for.'

A wary sense of peace had settled over her by the time the plane landed at Maraban's splendid new airport. But when she stepped out of the plane to the music being played by a military band, and a smiling older man stepped up to bow and address Zahir while a little girl in a fancy dress stepped nervously forward to present a bouquet of flowers to Saffy, she realised that he had been right to warn her that her life would radically change. Zahir introduced her and the man bowed very low. He was the prime minister of Maraban. A discovery that startled Saffy and embarrassed her, for she knew she should have spent more time boning up on the changes in the country that was to be her new home. She had assumed Zahir was a feudal king like his late father, but evidently Maraban now had an elected government as well.

The little girl was the prime minister's daughter and spoke English and Saffy, always at her best with children, bent down to chat to her, suddenly wondering whether the child she carried would be a boy or a girl. A little boy with Zahir's amazing eyes and love of the outdoors and action. Or a little girl, who liked to experiment with hair and make-up and clothes. Or a mix of both of them, which would be much more likely, Saffy acknowledged abstractedly.

A limousine carried them through the city streets, lined on either side by excited crowds, peering at the car. 'Do I have to wave or anything?' she asked uneasily.

'No, only smile to look as happy as a bride is popularly supposed to be,' Zahir murmured with a wry note in his dark deep voice, and she suspected that he was recalling the night they had just spent apart.

'Your people seem to be celebrating the fact that you've got married,' Saffy remarked.

'People are reassured by the concept of family and

continuity, as long as it doesn't include a man like my late father,' Zahir imparted drily, and then turned to look at her. 'Why do you never mention yours? I noticed he was not at the wedding and didn't like to ask because you never ever mentioned him five years ago. Is he dead?'

'No. Alive with a second wife and family. His divorce from my mother was very bitter,' Saffy confided. 'And he hasn't had anything to do with me since I was twelve years old when I did something...' her voice slowed and thickened with distress '...something he couldn't forgive.'

His black brows drew together and he regarded her keenly. 'What could you have done that would excuse such an outright rejection from a father of his own child? I can't believe you did anything worthy of such a punishment.'

Saffy was very pale and she compressed her lips. 'Then you'd be wrong.'

'Tell me...you can't give me only half of the story.'.

It was her second most shameful secret, Saffy reflected wretchedly, but one that there was no reason for her to keep from him as he was part of her family now and everyone else knew the facts. 'As you know, life was pretty rough where I grew up and my sisters and I were often left without supervision, so of course we got in with the wrong crowd,' she confided tightly, her skin already turning clammy with never-forgotten shame and guilt. 'I went joyriding in a stolen car with my twin. I didn't steal it *or* drive it but the car crashed. Her leg was badly damaged and she was left disabled and scarred for several years afterwards. She went through hell as a teenager. Luckily she was able to have surgery when she was older and she can walk normally again now. But the joyriders were my friends first and it was my fault. I'm the older twin and I should have been looking after her.'

'Saffy...' and it was the very first time he had used the family diminutive of her name, which made his intervention all the more effective as she turned her head in surprise, her clouded blue eyes meeting his. 'You were twelve years old. You did something wrong and you paid a heavy price—'

'No, *Emmie* did—' Saffy protested vehemently. 'Every morning for years she had to wake up and see her identical twin, walking, unscarred, *perfect* and, even though she's completely healed now, she's never been able to forgive me for what she went through during that period of her life. We both know I was to blame and that it should have been me who got hurt.'

'But you *were* hurt,' Zahir murmured gently. 'She was hurt in the body and you were hurt in the mind. You've carried the guilt for what happened ever since, haven't you?'

Tears were swimming in Saffy's eyes and she didn't trust herself to speak, so she nodded vigorously in agreement. All those years she had stood by watching her twin suffer, first in a wheelchair, then on crutches, struggling to fit in with other teenagers when she couldn't play sport or dance or do almost anything that they could.

'Accidents happen,' Zahir continued. 'You learned from the experience, didn't you?'

Saffy nodded wordlessly, a soundless sob thickening her throat and making it impossible to swallow.

'So what did your father do?'

'He said…he said I was evil and that he didn't want to know me any more.'

'And how did he treat Emmie?'

'He cut her out of his life as well. So, you see, that was my fault too.'

'No. He was a father and perhaps he used your mistakes as an excuse to absolve himself of responsibility for his twin daughters. No decent man would stay away from an injured child merely to punish her sibling.'

That was a truth that had evaded Saffy all her life to that point and it shook her because when Zahir put the episode in that light, she saw his view of it and it altered her own. Her father had conveniently rejected both his daughters. Although Emmie had been hurt, he hadn't even visited her in hospital, nor had he intervened when the twins were forced to enter foster care because their mother refused to take further responsibility for them. It had been Saffy's sister, Kat, who had been the three sisters' saviour, giving them a proper home and a loving caring environment, the first any of them had ever known.

'I appreciate you viewing the episode that way,' Saffy breathed in a muffled undertone. 'But Emmie can't see it like that. She still doesn't want anything to do with me.'

'As I've never met her, you'll have to talk to her about that. Put it out of your mind now,' Zahir urged, stunning dark golden eyes welded to her troubled face, a smile slashing his wide sensual mouth. 'and stop blaming yourself for something that was outside your control.'

Her spirits picked up as if a bubble of happiness had been released inside her. He knew what she had done and it hadn't shocked him or made him see her as a cruelly irresponsible and selfish person. And most miraculously of all, he had made her feel better with one smile. She gazed back at him, her heart thumping hard inside her chest, an agony of feeling squeezed tight inside her. She wanted so badly to touch him, could feel her breasts heavy, the tender tips straining inside her bra while a warm honeyed heat built between her legs. It was pure lust, she told herself defensively, watching his eyes flame gold, and lust was a practical basis for a practical marriage.

'If we weren't in view of hundreds of people, you would be horizontal,' Zahir purred hungrily, the erotic note in his sensual drawl tugging at her senses.

'As you said, we have all the time in the world,' Saffy burbled, relieved that he could still respond to her, *want* her. 'I did think that the way you behaved yesterday meant that, now that I'm pregnant, I had lost my appeal,' she told him baldly.

Zahir laughed with rich appreciation. 'Is that a joke?'

Saffy stiffened. 'No.'

'Knowing that's my baby inside you makes me want you more than ever,' he breathed with a husky sensual edge to his voice, surveying her in a way no woman could have misunderstood or doubted, his hunger unashamed.

Although her colour heightened, Saffy relaxed, reassured that she was still an object of desire. In reality, she wanted a great deal more from him, she acknowledged inwardly, but it was early days and she could be patient. After all, she loved him. She couldn't lie to herself any longer about that. She had married him because she wanted to be his wife again, not only because of the child she carried. She wasn't quite the clear-headed, unselfish person she had pretended to be inside her own mind, putting her child's needs first. She wanted Zahir, she *loved* Zahir, and somehow she was going to make their marriage work so well that he found her indispensable. Furthermore, she wasn't going to cripple herself with wounding suspicions about other women, past infidelities or indeed anything from that era, she swore fiercely to herself. This marriage was a new beginning, not a rerun of mistakes and misunderstandings made long ago.

CHAPTER NINE

THE ROYAL PALACE was a vast building dating back hundreds of years and extended and renovated by every successive generation of Zahir's family. Even from the outside Saffy could see changes everywhere she looked because the massive courtyard fronting the palace entrance, once a parking area for military vehicles and limousines, had been transformed into beautiful gardens full of graceful trees being industriously watered to keep them healthy in the heat. Glorious flowering shrubs bloomed in every direction and fountains fanned water to cool the air in terraced seating areas. The gardeners at work fell still and lowered their heads respectfully as the limo passed by. When the late King Fareed had driven past, everyone had fallen down on their knees at his insistence and she was relieved that Zahir had clearly brought an end to that kind of exaggerated subservience.

'It looks so different,' she commented as the limo drew up outside the huge arched entrance. 'Much more welcoming.'

'It's so big we initially thought of knocking it down

and constructing something more fit for purpose. After all, I don't live like my father with hundreds of servants and guards, but it *is* an historic building and, since the family only requires part of it to actually live in, the government uses one wing and official events are staged here. We will still have total privacy though,' he asserted. 'Don't worry about that. And, of course, you'll be free to redecorate and do anything you like with our wing of the palace. I want you to feel at home here this time.'

Saffy decided that she would pretty much come to like and accept any place Zahir called home. Besides, their baby had been conceived in a tent. A palatial tent, to be sure, but a tent nonetheless. Her lush mouth quirked at the recollection. That was a secret that would probably never be shared.

The domestic staff greeted them at the end of the long hall and she was given more flowers, which were in turn taken from her as if she could not be expected to carry anything for herself. Zahir closed a relaxed hand round hers and walked her into a big reception room where a man and a woman awaited them.

'Hayat…' Saffy greeted his sister, several years his senior, warmly, registering that the delicate youthful brunette she had once met was now a more rounded woman in her thirties, but she still had the same warm, friendly smile. Hayat was quick to kiss her on both cheeks and offer good wishes. Saffy had never got to know the older woman that well because when she had first been married to Zahir, Hayat and her husband had been living in Switzerland.

'And since he was only a boy when you last met him, this is my younger brother Akram.'

She would have known Zahir's brother immediately by his close resemblance to her husband, but she was not impervious to the look of hostility in his rather set face as he murmured a strictly polite welcome that was neither sociable nor encouraging. But Saffy kept the smile on her face, reminding herself that it was early days and that, after the divorce five years earlier, Akram might consider her a particularly bad match for his brother, the king. Or maybe Akram was less than impressed by the fact that she was already pregnant, although if that was the case he ought to remember that conception took two people, not one, she thought ruefully.

Zahir carried her off again, one hand closed round hers as if he was keen to retain physical contact and, certainly, she had no objection retaining that connection. She had never been in the wing of the palace he took her to, was happy to be invited to explore and was pleasantly surprised by how contemporary the décor was there. Back in the old dark days of King Fareed's occupation, the parts of the palace she had known had rejoiced in a preponderance of over-gilded furniture, brightly coloured wallpaper, fussy drapes and half-naked statues. But now all that was tasteless and garish had been swept away as though it had never been.

'Did your father ever live here?' she asked awkwardly.

'No,' Zahir said succinctly. 'I didn't want to occupy his wing at the front…too many bad memories. It's government offices now.'

'This is beautiful,' Saffy confided, brushing back filmy drapes and opening French windows that led out into a spacious garden courtyard full of lush colourful plants. 'It will be perfect for the baby to play in.'

'One last place to show you,' Zahir murmured, tugging her impatiently back indoors to walk her down the corridor, while she tried to compute the sheer number of rooms that she now had the right to regard as part of her new home. He flung open the double doors at the foot like a showman. 'Our room. I had it freshly decorated.'

Our room, she repeated inwardly, thinking that phrase, which once had unnerved her, now had a good, solid, reassuring sound to it. The big room was breathtaking in the morning sunshine, furnished with a simply huge bed dressed in white and covered with more pillows and cushions than anyone would ever want to move before slipping between the sheets. Masses of white flowers filled several vases and perfumed the air with their abundance. The effect was light, bright and designer chic. Twin bathrooms led off the bedroom, one with a family-sized Jacuzzi in the corner.

'I'm already picturing you in there,' Zahir muttered huskily from behind her, his breath warming her cheek as he settled his lean hands on her rounded hips.

'Are you indeed?' Sliding round to look up at him, Saffy lifted her hands to his face and curved them to his exotic cheekbones. Dear heaven, those eyes of his got to her every time, she conceded dizzily as he bent his handsome dark head and circled her lush mouth slowly, teasingly with his own and her heart skipped a beat. 'I'll only get in with company.'

His cell phone hummed and Zahir winced. 'Hold that thought,' he urged, digging it out of his pocket to speak in his own language.

And that fast the moment of intimacy was over. He inclined his head at an apologetic angle and told her that something needed his attention and he would see her later. Saffy suppressed her disappointment, conceding that their lives would often be interrupted by his duties and knowing she would have to get used to the fact. She returned to exploring their wing of the palace. A manservant brought her luggage. There was a complete dream of a clothing closet installed in the room next door and she smiled, smoothing shoe shelves and glancing into what could only be custom-built units. Knowing Zahir must have ensured that so much was prepared for her in advance gave her a warm feeling deep down inside.

A maid brought her tea and tiny cakes and she sat out in the tranquil courtyard garden below the shade of the palm trees, enjoying the fading afternoon heat and the play of shadows through the palm fronds. For the first time in a long time she felt at peace. Acknowledging her feelings for Zahir had eased her worst insecurities and put paid to her frantic changes of mood because now she knew what lay behind her reactions. They were husband and wife and she was carrying their first child and she was happy. Happy, she thought wryly, unable to recall when she had last felt so happy or indeed an intensity of any emotion: only around Zahir. Had she always still loved him? Had it been his haunting image that prevented her from ever experiencing a strong attraction to another man? Regardless of what had happened between them, she had retained past memories of Zahir that were still clear as day in her mind. He had referred to her once as his 'first love' and she knew she wanted to be his first and *only* love, but the clock still couldn't be turned back. And nor in many ways would Saffy have wanted to achieve that impossibility, not if it meant returning to the uninformed, bewildered teenager she had been, incapable of consummating her marriage and having to live within the confines of the repressive regime of the late King Fareed.

Zahir phoned her full of apologies to say that he could not join her before dinner. He reappeared, vital and startlingly handsome, to study her where she sat reading on the terrace. She smiled at him, blue eyes sparkling, and his winged brows pleated in surprise. 'I thought you'd be furious with me for leaving you alone all afternoon,' he admitted ruefully.

And Saffy laughed. 'I'm not eighteen any more,' she reminded him gently. 'And I understand that you have responsibilities you can't escape.'

'But not the very first day you arrive. In that spirit, I have blocked off two weeks at the end of the month purely for us,' Zahir told her, his features suddenly very serious in cast. 'We can travel, stay here, do whatever you like, but there will no other demands on our time.'

Saffy was impressed that he had already foreseen the necessity for them to formally make space in their schedules to spend time together as a couple. It was an effort and an opportunity he had not tried to organise five years earlier and she appreciated it. A pretty fabulous three-course meal was served to them in the dining room. There was evidently a chef in charge of the kitchens and one out to impress. While they ate, Zahir shared his ambition to promote Maraban as a tourist destination and he asked her if she would be interested in helping to put together a public relations film to show off some of Maraban's main attractions.

'We have beaches, archaeological sites, mountains,' Zahir told her persuasively. 'You could present it. You're accustomed to being in front of the cameras.'

'Not in a speaking role, at least only occasionally.' But Saffy was pleased to be offered the chance to do something useful. 'I haven't been to any of those places though.'

Zahir frowned at the unspoken reminder that his father's determination to conceal their marriage had left her virtually imprisoned within the palace walls. 'Your eyes will be fresh then, your observations and expectations more realistic. We have a lot to learn about what tourists want. We don't have many marketing people here,' he confided. 'In fact Maraban would still be floundering and trapped in past mistakes if thousands of our former citizens hadn't responded to my appeal to come home after my father's regime fell. Many professionals returned from abroad to enable us to tackle the challenge of bringing our country into the twenty-first century.'

'It's wonderful that people chose to come back and help,' Saffy murmured, loving the gravity of his lean strong face, the warmth and concern he could not hide when he spoke about the country of his birth.

'But not half as wonderful as having you here with me again,' Zahir countered, dark golden eyes welded to her as he rose from his chair. 'Will you come to bed with me now, Your Majesty?'

'Call me Queenie—I'm never going to get used to the other. In answer to your question, I don't know...' Saffy angled her head to one side, pretending to think it over even though her heart was racing like a marathon runner's. 'Last night you were a no-show.'

Faint colour darkened his cheekbones. 'On board our flight, I didn't think I'd be welcome.'

'Put it this way—I wouldn't have kicked you out of bed,' Saffy confided, turning pink.

With a flashing smile of satisfaction, Zahir crossed the room and snatched her bodily up off the carpet into his arms to carry her down the corridor, a process accompanied by much giggling from Saffy. Half-way towards their bedroom he started kissing her and an arrow of sweet, piercing heat slivered between her thighs, smothering her amusement and awakening her body to desire.

'Being alone with you is all I've thought about all

day,' Zahir admitted, settling her down on the gigantic bed, which she noted was already clear of cushions and turned down in readiness for their occupation. Evidently the staff might be well acquainted with the habits of newly married couples.

As he cast off his robes and she kicked off her shoes Saffy smiled at his honesty. 'One-track mind.'

'*Always*…with you.' Zahir nuzzled against her slender throat, kissing and licking a sensitive spot below her ear that made her quiver and tightened her sensitive nipples. Then he groaned. 'I need a shave—'

Saffy grabbed him before he could spring back off the bed. '*Not* right now,' she told him squarely.

Zahir laughed. 'I don't want to scratch you.'

'Face facts. I won't agree to you going anywhere right at this minute,' Saffy told him, smoothing appreciative palms up over his broad muscular chest and then down very, very slowly and appreciatively over his six-pack abs. 'This is my time and I'm holding on tight to you.'

In the moonlight, Zahir's lean features were taut. 'You mean that?'

Saffy's fingers trailed daringly lower and closed around his bold erection.

With a roughened groan of satisfaction, Zahir flung himself back against the pillows. 'You're absolutely right. Nothing would move me right now.'

Saffy leant over him, her mane of hair trailing across his abdomen. He said something in Arabic. She pressed her lips to the tiny brown disc of a male nipple and moved in a southerly direction, taking her time as she kissed and stroked her way down his beautiful bronzed body.

'This is our wedding night…' Zahir muttered thickly. 'I should be doing this to you.'

'My turn later…right now, I'm in charge,' Saffy whispered just before she found him with her mouth and his hands lodged firmly into her hair, his hips rising to assist her, and an exclamation of intense pleasure was wrenched from him. Proud of her own boldness, no longer ashamed of the desire he roused in her, Saffy was thoroughly enjoying herself.

She loved having him in her power, revelled in every response he couldn't control and experienced a deep sense of achievement when he could no longer stand her teasing caresses and he dragged her up to him and flipped her over to ravage her lush lips with an almost savage kiss.

Making love to Zahir turned her on and no sooner had he registered that fact than he rose over her, all masculine, dominant power and energy, and thrust his engorged shaft into the silky wet tightness of her inner channel. She cried out in delight and then he was moving and stretching her, ramping up her level of excitement to an almost unbearable degree. It had never occurred to her that slow and deep could be as thrilling as fast and hard, but he wouldn't let her urge him on and control the pace.

'No, this we do *my* way,' Zahir growled, flexing his hips, sending a shiver of exquisite sensitivity over her entire skin surface, her nipples straining as he shifted position and angle to torture her more.

He kept her straining on the edge of climax for a long time and the ripples of growing excitement were engulfing her like a flood when, in receipt of one final driving thrust, she found a wild, scorching release that shattered her into shaking, sobbing weightlessness, utterly drained by the joy of the experience. She lay there for a long time afterwards, wrapped in his arms, steeped in pure pleasure, marvelling that they were together again.

'Now perhaps you'll consider telling me what or *who* transformed you in the bedroom from the terrified girl I remember into the woman you are now,' Zahir urged in a roughened undertone that nonetheless shockwaved through her like a sudden clap of thunder.

In receipt of that request, a little shudder of repulsion travelled through Saffy's suddenly ferociously tense body. No, she could not do that; no, she could not risk sharing what had happened to her lest it destroy the new bonds they had created. She could feel him waiting for her to speak, literally *willing* her to speak in that dreadful expectant silence. As the silence continued and she failed to respond the strong, protective arms wrapped round her tensed, loosened and then carefully withdrew and he shifted his lean, powerful body away from hers, forging a separation between them that she could feel aching through every fibre she possessed.

Zahir wasn't giving her a choice and he wasn't about to conveniently drop the subject for the sake of peace either, she recognised wretchedly. He wanted to know;

he was determined to know and he had a will of iron that would chip away at her obstinacy day after day. He wouldn't let it go and the distance that would create between them would provide fertile ground in which suspicion might well fester. Would he then start to doubt that he was truly her baby's father? Would he wonder if he had really been her only lover?

Stinging tears stung Saffy's eyes and trickled down her cheeks in the darkness. He was always so honest; he never seemed afraid of anything, never seemed to worry about how other people saw him. Why couldn't she be the same? Why couldn't she just spill it all out and stop worrying about how it might damage his view of her? But Saffy couldn't find an answer to the never-tell-anyone barrier that existed inside her mind. The therapist had had a lot of trouble getting her to talk and finally she had had hypnotherapy to overcome what she was too afraid and ashamed to remember, and only then, in possession of full knowledge, had she found it possible to move forward...

CHAPTER TEN

BREAKFAST FOR SAFFY and Zahir the following morning was an almost silent affair. Zahir, being Zahir of course, was scrupulously polite and yet in every glance, every intonation Saffy imagined she heard condemnation, suspicion, doubt that she could be trusted as he believed he should be able to trust his wife. Nausea stirred in her stomach as she contemplated the piece of toast clasped between her fingers and with a stifled apology she fled for the nearest bathroom to lose what little she had eaten.

Afterwards, weak and with hot, perspiring skin she lay down on the bed, relishing the restorative coolness of the air conditioning wafting over her.

Zahir strode through the bedroom door, stunning dark golden eyes intent on the picture she presented. 'With all the flowers surrounding you here you look like the Sleeping Beauty...'

Saffy parted pink lips. 'But this doesn't feel like a fairy tale,' she whispered apologetically because if there had ever been a romantic male, it was Zahir. And how on earth could a romantic male ever come to terms with something as ugly as her biggest secret?

'I've phoned Hayat's obstetrician.'

'Why the heck did you do that?'

'You're sick. You need medical attention,' Zahir informed her with a stubborn angle to his jaw line.

'Being sick in early pregnancy is very common and not something to make a fuss about,' Saffy countered steadily.

'I shouldn't have tired you out last night,' Zahir responded tight-mouthed, his beautiful eyes shaded by his outrageously lush black lashes.

Saffy thrust her hands down onto the mattress to lift herself up into sitting position. 'That's got nothing to do with this—this is only my body struggling to adapt to being newly pregnant and it's normal.'

'I will stop worrying only when the doctor tells me to do so. I'm responsible for looking after you,' Zahir asserted, unimpressed by her argument. 'And while I realise that you're not feeling like it, you must make an effort to eat some breakfast to keep your strength up.'

And the boss has spoken, Saffy tagged on in silence to that speech as Zahir stalked out of the door again. He did *care* that she wasn't feeling well, she assured herself ruefully. It wasn't love but it was concern, but for how long would she even retain that hold on him if she continued to keep her secrets? Naturally he was curious, naturally sooner or later he would need to know the truth about her past. For the first time she accepted that telling Zahir the truth was unavoidable and a bridge she would eventually have to cross.

Zahir's sister, Hayat, accompanied the consultant, who had tended her through her pregnancies. A well-built older man with a studious manner, he was calm and practical and exactly what Saffy needed to reinforce her belief that a little nausea was not serious cause for concern.

'The baby's father is very worried about your health,' the doctor declared. 'It is a challenge of civility to tell a king he must not worry unduly.'

Hayat was waiting outside to ask Saffy to join her for tea. Dressed in a light summer dress in shades of blue, Saffy accompanied her sister-in-law to the rear of the palace complex where she and her husband and children lived. Her husband, Rahim, was a senior doctor at the city hospital and their three little girls occupied much of Hayat and Saffy's conversation until a maid arrived to take the children out to the gardens to play.

Tea with tiny sweet cakes was served on a shaded balcony.

'My brother needs to learn to say no,' Hayat told Saffy firmly. 'The same day he brings you home a bride he was immediately dragged into some government squabble about security concerns and forced to abandon you. You will quickly discover that Zahir doesn't know how to say no to the demands made on his time.'

Saffy simply smiled, warmed by the frank tongue that Hayat appeared to share with her brother. 'Zahir was always very conscientious. Thank you for being so welcoming, Hayat. I appreciate it.'

'I know how much you and Zahir went through when you were married five years ago and our people now have a very good idea as well,' Hayat commented, her brown eyes level and serious. 'Zahir was wise when he chose to issue a public statement, admitting that he was remarrying the woman whom his father once forced him to divorce.'

Saffy stiffened in surprise at that revelation. 'I had no idea there had been any statement made about our marriage!' she exclaimed.

'Or that now my brother, the king, is forced to tell *lies* in public to protect *you?*' another louder voice interposed from the doorway behind them and both women's heads whipped around in astonishment at the interruption.

'Akram!' Hayat snapped in a warning tone at her youngest brother before turning back to Saffy with her face flushed and her expression uneasy to say, 'Please excuse me for a moment.'

But Zahir's volatile kid brother had worked up too much of a head of steam to be denied the confrontation with his brother's wife that his temper clearly craved. He concentrated his attention on Saffy, who was already starting to rise from her chair in dismay. 'You walked out on my brother—you *deserted* him after all he had endured to keep you as a wife against our father's wishes!' he accused with loathing. 'Zahir was imprisoned, tortured and beaten for your benefit and then you threw your marriage away by divorcing him when he needed your loyalty most!'

Her expression distraught, Hayat was pleading with her angry brother to keep quiet while simultaneously yanking on his arm in an unsuccessful effort to physically drag him away.

Saffy could barely part her numb lips. She was in serious shock from Akram's ringing condemnation of her behaviour. And what on earth was he talking about? Imprisoned, tortured, *beaten? Zahir?*

'I will deal with this…' and another more familiar voice intervened, cutting across the row going on between Hayat and Akram with commanding force.

Trembling, Saffy focused on Zahir where he stood like a bronzed statue in the centre of the light, airy reception room, coldly surveying his squabbling siblings. He spoke in his own language at length to Akram and Hayat backed off, dropping her head apologetically. Whatever Zahir told his brother, Akram turned his head in consternation to stare back at Saffy with frowning disbelief. He took a half-step towards her and muttered uncomfortably, 'I am very sorry. It seems I got everything wrong.'

'Yes, Zahir divorced me,' Saffy pointed out ruefully.

'Even so, I should never have spoken to you in that way or approached you in a temper. It was not my business,' Akram mumbled, his face very flushed, his discomfiture in Zahir's thunderous presence pronounced. 'Over the years it seems I reached the wrong conclusions and, as my brother has reminded me, I was never party to the true facts of what happened between you.'

An uneasy silence fell. Zahir was still glaring angrily at his kid brother.

'No harm done,' Saffy said awkwardly, keen to dispel the tension. 'I assume that Zahir has told you what really happened and that you no longer think so badly of me. Now, if you would all excuse me...'

'Where are you going?' Zahir demanded.

'Only for a walk. I'd like to be alone for a while,' she muttered tightly.

'I will accompany you,' Zahir pronounced.

'No...I only want a minute alone,' Saffy whispered pleadingly, because she was thinking about what Akram had hurled at her and reaching the worst possible conclusions. Zahir had been punished by his father for defying him by marrying her? Why had that possibility never occurred to her before? Why had she been so wrapped up in her own misery that it had never occurred to her that Zahir might be dealing with bad things too? But, imprisoned, tortured, beaten...surely not? Was that possible? Would his father have subjected his son to such brutal intimidation? According to his reputation, King Fareed had been responsible for many atrocities. She thought of Zahir's appallingly scarred back and a sense of cold fear of the unknown and of such cruelty infiltrated her. But if Zahir had suffered like that, why hadn't he told her?

When Saffy actually focused enough to recognise where her wandering feet had carried her, she realised that she was back in the old part of the palace where she had once lived. She walked down a dim corridor and cast open the door of the room that had once been theirs. It shook her that it was still furnished the same, untouched by time or alteration, and she walked in with a compulsive shiver of remembrance of the past.

A thousand images engulfed her all at once and she reeled from memories of Zahir watching her with wary eyes, his silences, sudden absences and his refusal to answer questions. Had he been hiding stuff from her that she should have guessed? Was Akram telling the truth? She couldn't bear that suspicion, wasn't sure she could ever live with any discovery that painful...

'I should have had this place cleared...' Zahir murmured from behind her. 'But I used to come here to think about you.'

Saffy turned round, her face pale as milk, her eyes nakedly vulnerable. 'When? After the divorce? I think you need to start talking, Zahir...and maybe I do too,' she acknowledged unevenly.

'After I married you, my brother Omar asked me if I was insane to challenge our father to that extent,' Zahir admitted with curt reluctance. 'But at first I genuinely had no idea what I was dealing with: Omar had protected me too much. He kept a lot of secrets. I was the younger son, the junior army officer, and I wasn't part of the inner circle of people who knew what a monster my father had become on a diet of unfettered power.'

'So, you must have regretted marrying me rather quickly,' Saffy assumed, searching the lean strong features she loved for every passing nuance of expression and sinking down on the edge of the bed where she had often cried her heart out with loneliness.

His handsome mouth hardened. 'I only ever regretted the unnatural lifestyle which our marriage inflicted on you. I had no regrets on my own behalf.'

'That's a kind thing to say but it can't be the way you really felt.'

'I loved you more than life,' Zahir breathed starkly. 'My mistake was in rebelling against my father and bringing you back here to become the equivalent of a hostage. I should have married you and left you in London where you would be safe, but I was too selfish to do that.'

Loved you more than life. The declaration rippled through her like an unexpected benediction, steadying her nerves. 'I loved you too. You weren't selfish. I wouldn't have agreed to being left behind in London.'

'But you didn't know what you were getting into here any more than I did.' Face grave, Zahir compressed his lips. 'Omar had been married five years and he still had no child. Our father was impatient to see the next generation in the family born.'

'That must have put a lot of pressure on Omar and Azel.'

'More on Omar for the lack of fertility was his, *not* hers but I didn't learn that until shortly before Omar... *died*.' He spoke that last word with curious emphasis. 'My older brother's secret was that he had discovered he was unable to father a child and he was afraid to tell our father lest he was passed over in the succession stakes in favour of me. Omar was always the ambitious one,' Zahir told her heavily. 'Unfortunately for him, our father had run out of patience. He demanded that Omar either set Azel aside or take a second wife.'

Saffy was shocked. 'And that was the background to *our* marriage?'

'Our father was doubly enraged when I married you without permission because my marriage to a suitable woman would have been the next step on his agenda.'

'And of course I got in the way of his plans,' Saffy completed. 'Yet you thought he would eventually accept me.'

'I was wrong,' Zahir admitted grittily. 'I was much more naïve than I thought I was about what our father was really like. I never dreamt he would be as vicious with his sons as he was to some of our people. How adolescent was such innocence in a grown man?'

'Everybody wants to think the best of their parents,' Saffy told him with rueful understanding. 'I don't blame you for getting it wrong.'

'The year we were married was the year my father went over the edge. Although I was unaware of it, he had become a regular drug user and suffered from violent rages. From the first day you arrived he wanted me to divorce you...and the sensible act would have been to surrender to greater force, but I was never sensible about you.'

Her heart was beating in what felt uncomfortably like the foot of her throat. 'Greater force?' she queried suspiciously. 'If even half of what Akram suggested happened to you, I have the right to know about it. *Were* you imprisoned? Tortured? *Beaten?*'

Zahir stared levelly back at her, not a muscle moving on his bronzed handsome face, his mouth an unsmiling line. 'I could curse Akram, though he spoke out of ignorance. This is a conversation I never wanted to have with you…'

Saffy was trembling. 'You're telling me that your father—your own father—did do that stuff to you?' she prompted sickly. 'That you weren't away on army manoeuvres when you disappeared for weeks on end?'

Zahir gave confirmation with a grudging jerk of his chin.

And Saffy just closed her eyes, because all of a sudden she couldn't bear to look at him when she had excelled at being such a blind, childish fool all the months they had been man and wife the first time around. He had reappeared after those apparent military trips, filthy, often visibly bruised and cut, always having lost weight…and not once had she questioned the condition he was in, not once had she suspected that he had been brutally ill-treated while he was away from her and prevented from returning from her. In her little cocoon the very fact he was a prince had made entertaining such a suspicion too incredible to even consider. She had assumed that soldiers led a rough and ready life and that such trips were organised to be as realistic and tough as real warfare. And he had never told her, never once breathed a word of what was being done to him, never once sought her sympathy or support…

'Why didn't you tell me?' she asked thickly, tears thickening her throat and creating a huge lump there.

'I didn't want to upset you. There was nothing you could have done to stop it. Omar was correct. I should never have brought you to Maraban. Our father was a madman and he was out of control, incapable of accepting any form of opposition. It was all or nothing and once I defied him he was determined to break me.'

'And all over *me*…all because you married me,' Saffy muttered, her distress growing by the second as she looked back on her colossally ignorant and oblivious self at the age of eighteen. Little wonder he had ducked her questions, embraced silence, never knowing when he would be with her or torn from her side again.

'That whole year you were the only thing that kept me going,' Zahir informed her harshly. *'Look at me.'*

'No!' Saffy unfroze finally and flew upright. 'I have to think about this on my own!'

As she tried to brush past him he closed a hand round a slim forearm. 'I told you I would tell no more lies or half-truths but I never wanted you to know about that period of my life!'

'Oh, I know that…Mr Macho-I-suffer-in-silence!' Saffy condemned chokily, her increasing distress clawing at her control. 'So when you came back here to me after suffering gross mistreatment and allowed me to shout at you and complain that I was bored and lonely?

Just what I need to know to feel like the biggest bitch ever created!'

And, tears streaming down her distraught face, Saffy fled, in need of privacy. How could he do that to her? How could he not have told her? How could he have allowed her to find out all that from his resentful brother? She had known King Fareed wasn't a pleasant or popular man, but she had had no idea that he was a drug-abusing tyrant capable of torturing his own son if he was disobedient! What an idiot she must have been not to have guessed that something so dreadful was going on! How could she ever forgive herself for that? *You were the only thing that kept me going.* Why was he still trying to make her feel better by saying that sort of rubbish? He'd been stuck in a virtually sexless marriage while being regularly punished for rebelling against his father's dictates. And not once had she suspected anything. Was she stupid, utterly stupid, to have been so unseeing?

Saffy took refuge in their new bedroom, which was comfortably removed from the suffocating memories of the older accommodation they had once occasionally shared. She was remembering the condition of Zahir's back, thinking, although she didn't want to, of him being whipped, beaten up, *hurt* and all on her behalf. Zahir with his pride and his intrinsic sense of decency! She ran to the bathroom and heaved but nothing came up and she hugged the vanity unit to stay upright, surveying her tousled reflection with stricken accusing eyes.

How could you not know? How could you not see what he was going through?

'This is why I never wanted you to know. I didn't want to see you hurt because all of it was my fault…'

Saffy spun round. He stood in the doorway, lean and bronzed and gorgeous in black jeans and a white shirt, so much the guy she loved and admired and cared about. 'How was it your fault?' she scissored back at him incredulously.

'I married you. I brought you back here with me. I placed both of us in a foolish and vulnerable position,' Zahir stated grimly. 'I will never forgive myself for that.'

'You should've divorced me the minute the punishments started!' Saffy launched back at him. 'How could you be so stubborn that you went through that just for me?'

A faint shadow of a smile that struck her as impossible in the circumstances curved his wide sensual mouth. 'I loved you…I couldn't give you up.'

'I wouldn't have let you go through that if I'd known! How could you still want me?' she sobbed in disbelief. 'I wasn't even able to give you sex!'

'The sex was the least of it. Believe me, at the time, consummating our marriage was not my biggest challenge.' His stunning golden eyes lowered from her shaken face and he held out a hand until she grasped it, allowing him to pull her closer. 'But I couldn't seek help or advice for us either. Had anyone known we had those problems my father would have had yet another reason to want you out of my life…'

Saffy dragged in a quivering breath, still reeling from what she had learned. Eyes wet, she pushed her face against his shoulder, drinking in the scent of his sun-warmed flesh, the faint evocative tang that was uniquely his, which made her feel vaguely intoxicated. She was addicted to him, so pathetically *addicted.* 'Thank heaven you finally had the sense to divorce me and give the dreadful man what he wanted.'

'That was probably the one and only unselfish thing I ever did while I was married to you, the only thing I *ever* did solely for you and not for me,' Zahir muttered roughly above her down-bent head, his lips brushing across her brow in a calming gesture. 'I'm not the saint you seem to think. I made appalling errors of judgement.'

Her forehead furrowing, she looked up at him 'Such as?'

'Bringing you into Maraban five years ago,' he specified. 'Three months after Omar's death, I found out that he had been murdered…'

'What?' Shattered by that statement, she stared up at him.

'One of the generals told me the truth because the most senior army personnel were becoming nervous about my father's reign of terror. Omar was beaten up by my father's henchmen and he died from a head injury. The car crash was simply a cover-up. It was then that I realised that my father really had gone beyond the hope of return,' Zahir revealed rawly.

'Oh…my…word,' Saffy framed sickly. 'Are you sure?'

'One hundred per cent.' Zahir compressed his lips. 'That's when I appreciated that keeping you in Maraban was sheer insanity when my father wanted rid of you. I didn't have the power to protect you. I was putting your life at risk by refusing to divorce you. I was making you a target in my father's eyes. I'm ashamed it took Omar's death to make me accept that if I couldn't keep you safe, I *had* to let you go….'

Saffy's heart was beating very loudly in her eardrums and she drifted dizzily away from him on weak legs to drop heavily down on a sofa in the corner of their room. 'So, that's why the divorce came out of nowhere at me. You honestly thought I was in danger. Why didn't you tell me the truth then, Zahir?'

'The truth would have terrified you and I was ashamed that I could not even keep myself safe, never mind my wife. But that was also the moment that, in losing you, my father finally lost my loyalty. I could never have forgiven him for what he had done to Omar, but losing you was excruciating,' he completed gruffly, dropping down on his knees in front of her and momentarily lowering his dark head down onto her lap. 'You have no idea how much I loved you, what strength it took to give you up, knowing, having to accept that it was the *only* thing I could do…'

As he admitted that stinging tears were rolling down Saffy's face. She had never dreamt that she could feel such pain on someone else's behalf and yet when Zahir talked of how much it had hurt to divorce her, it was as if a giant black hole of unhappiness opened up inside her and cracked her heart right down the middle. Her fingers delved into his luxuriant black hair, delving, smoothing. 'I loved you too...I loved you so much. I don't think I even understood how much I needed you in my life until we were forced apart,' she confided jaggedly.

'I tried to contact you after my father died and the fighting was finished,' Zahir told her grimly as he lifted his handsome dark head and leapt back upright to pace restively. 'I spoke to your sister, Kat.'

Saffy was stunned. 'She didn't tell me.'

Zahir grimaced. 'Kat pleaded with me to leave you alone. She said you had just got your life back together, that you were working, making friends and that the last thing you needed was to see me again,' Zahir recalled, tight-mouthed at the recollection.

Saffy felt as if someone had walked over her grave. How could the sister she loved have got her so wrong? The divorce had broken her heart but she had still loved Zahir and would have moved heaven and earth to see him again. 'She shouldn't have interfered.'

'On that score we'll have to disagree.' Zahir surprised her with that response. 'Sadly, even though I didn't like what Kat had to say, she was right.'

'No, she was wrong,' Saffy contradicted.

'You were far too young to deal with what I was dealing with then on top of the other problems we had and Maraban had. You needed the time to live the normal life you should have enjoyed before we married,' Zahir contended. 'I can see that now but I couldn't see it at the time. I simply wanted you back the minute it would have been safe to bring you back…'

Tears trickled down Saffy's cheeks. 'I would've come back to you,' she whispered shakily.

'You would've walked away from those magazine covers and your face everywhere?' Zahir prompted dubiously.

'Yes, it was never that important to me. It was the means to make a living and not be a burden on my sister.'

Zahir bent down and grasped her hands to raise her. 'But we work better now because we're older and wiser.'

A shadow crossed her lovely face. 'And, of course, you're much more experienced.'

He paled, his strong bone structure tightening. 'After our *mutual* failure, I was afraid I had become…impotent. I had lost all confidence,' he confided in a grudging undertone, tension and shame etched in every line of his strong face. 'I knew I had to get past my obsession with you because you were no longer mine. My father sent me abroad before the civil war broke out. Ironically he was trying to reward me for divorcing you…'

Saffy lifted her fingers and gently smoothed the stubborn angle of his jaw. 'It's all right. I can't say I don't mind because that would be a lie, but I understand why it happened.'

His beautiful dark eyes narrowed and centred intently on her solemn face. 'Then isn't it time you explained how that miracle happened for you? You insist there hasn't been another man but—'

'That was the truth.' Her wandering fingers strayed to his wide sensual lower lip to silence him. 'I wanted to be normal in the bedroom and I went to see a specialist to find out what was wrong with me. I was told that I suffered from a condition called vaginismus, which is an involuntary tightening of the pelvic muscles, often triggered by some trauma in the past. My inability to relax, the panic attacks when you tried to touch me were all part of it,' she explained, doggedly pushing herself on to spill what had lain behind her deepest vulnerability. 'I went for therapy but it wasn't until I had hypnotherapy that I discovered what had triggered my phobia about that part of my body...'

Zahir held her back from him, his shrewd gaze welded to her troubled face and the sheen of perspiration already dampening her upper lip. 'Tell me—there should be nothing you can't tell me.'

'I was abused by one of my mother's boyfriends when I was a child,' Saffy framed shakily, tears welling up in her eyes because she could not bring herself to look and see how he was reacting to that unsavoury news. 'I suppose I was lucky he didn't rape me, but then he was never able to get me alone for very long. He threatened me. He said that if I told Mum, she wouldn't believe me, and he said Emmie and Topsy would have to take my place.'

Zahir swore in his own language and gripped her

shoulders. 'Please tell me that you went to your mother for help.'

A taut expression set Saffy's face. 'I did but my abuser was right—Mum refused to believe me and punished me for even opening the subject. My abuser was a well-off professional man with a name for being a womaniser and there was no way my mother was going to give him up or suspect him on only the strength of my word.'

Zahir pushed up her chin. 'What age were you?'

'Seven.' Saffy gazed up into his furious eyes and shivered. 'I couldn't stop him, Zahir, but I knew it was wrong.'

Zahir almost crushed her in his arms. 'Is that the impression I'm giving you? That it was somehow your fault that some filthy pervert abused your trust? That's *not* how I feel. I'm furious the bastard got away with it, furious your mother wouldn't listen to you, furious I wasn't there to prevent it happening in the first place!' he spelt out in a savage undertone.

'You're angry.'

'But *not* with you, with the people who have hurt you and let you down, even though I'm one of their number,' he muttered, his breathing fracturing as he scooped her up and brought her carefully down on the bed with him, holding her close to every line of his long, lean physique. 'Facing the fact that you'd been abused must have been very difficult for you.'

'Apparently it's quite common for children to suppress memories of that kind of assault,' Saffy whispered unevenly, reassured by the solid thump of his heart against her breast and the reality that he was hugging her without demonstrating any symptoms of revulsion towards her. 'I felt horrible but, on one level, it was a relief to find out what had made me the way I was. I knew I'd never be able to have another relationship until I could overcome my problems.'

'I wish I'd known. What treatment did you have?'

'I had loads of supportive counselling and then a physical intervention,' Saffy explained hesitantly. 'I had muscle relaxants injected to prevent the contractions and a dilator was inserted while I was still unconscious. For a long time I slept with it inserted overnight...' As Zahir looked down at her, her face was burning. 'I had to learn to accept my own body and to touch myself. I'd always avoided that without ever wondering why. I assumed I was just very fastidious, I didn't know I suffered from an actual phobia until we got married and it all went wrong. But after I had completed the treatment I did hope to find a lover once I'd worked through all the recovery steps.'

'And why didn't you do that?' Zahir demanded, stunning dark golden eyes pinned to her. 'I shouldn't have thought that would have been a challenge.'

'You'd be surprised. I not only wanted a man who attracted me, but also one whom I *cared* something about. Having waited so long and gone through so much to find the answer to my problems, I didn't want just anyone!' Saffy explained with spirit. 'Unfortunately the right guy didn't appear. To most of the men I met, I would only have been a trophy. I wanted more than that from a man. I believed I deserved more than that.'

His lush black lashes semi-screened his glittering scrutiny, colour lying in a hard line along his fabulous cheekbones. 'Then how on earth did you contrive to settle for me again?'

Saffy stiffened. 'I was still very attracted to you… don't know why,' she dared to pronounce, watching his amazing eyes smoulder at that challenge into glowing golden flames. 'I told myself that being with you didn't mean anything to me emotionally and that I was simply using you to get rid of my virginity.'

Zahir nodded very slowly and then bent his head to steal a kiss that made her head spin, and her fingers clutched frantic handfuls of his luxuriant black hair. The pressure of his mouth combined with the penetration of his tongue was an intoxicating thrill, so that when he lifted his head again, separating them, she frowned.

'I told myself a lot of lies that night in the tent as well. I couldn't admit how I still felt about you,' he confided with a hard twist of his mouth. 'In fact in the time we were divorced I had grown unreasonably and unjustly bitter.'

'Bitter?' she queried.

'Bitter that I'd loved and lost you and that you appeared to be having a hell of a good time without me. Even worse, I couldn't forget you,' he confessed harshly. 'There you were in my sister's magazines, which she was always leaving lying around, seemingly enjoying a party lifestyle with various different men. I was angry and jealous… There, I have said it at last! I wanted you back from the moment I lost you and I never changed towards you. I loved you five years ago and I love you even more now…'

'You…*do?*' Saffy was enchanted by that admission and the ferocious fervent force with which he spoke and studied her.

'I love you and I always will.' Zahir groaned because the wife he adored was not a patient woman and she was stroking her hand down his taut, powerful thigh with rousing intent.

'I love you too… I didn't stop loving you either,' Saffy confided. 'But I was too proud to admit that. At first, I wanted you to believe I'd had other lovers.'

'It wouldn't have mattered if you had had. I would still love you. I've grown up too,' Zahir declared. 'Circumstances tore us apart.'

'But you brought us back together again.' Saffy scored a fingernail along the rippling muscle of one thigh, loving his instant response to her provocation. 'You kidnapped me.'

'I also asked you to be my mistress. I'm ashamed of that,' he said bluntly. 'But I wanted you any way I could get you… I couldn't face losing you again but my behaviour was inexcusable.'

Saffy stared down at him and suddenly grinned, unable to hide her amusement. 'But that behaviour was very much *you*. You can't fight what you are inside: direct, bold, passionate. I couldn't believe you still wanted me that much after our disastrous year together.'

'I honestly did believe that it was *I* who had failed *you* in the bedroom,' Zahir told her tautly. 'I assumed my clumsiness and ignorance had scared you, that I'd hurt you, given you a *fear* of intimacy.'

'No...no, it wouldn't have mattered who I was with, it would have been the same, but another man might not have had your patience,' she argued, her eyes not leaving his for a second as, drawn like a moth to a flame, she slowly lowered her mouth to his. 'You were very kind and understanding when you must have been hugely sexually frustrated.'

It was Zahir's turn to smile. 'No, you took care of me in other ways and I had few complaints.'

Saffy tensed. 'Doesn't knowing about the...er... abuse turn you off?'

'No, it makes you even more worthy of being the love of my life. I know how strong you must be to have got through that and dealt with it.' With gentle fingers he smoothed a stray strand of golden hair from her brow. 'I know how hard I had to work coming to terms with what was done to me while I was imprisoned by my father...'

'I still can't stand the thought of that,' she admitted chokily, her eyes filming over.

'Omar and I were raised like spoilt little rich kids with titles. Being powerless and a victim taught me a lot that I needed to learn for the benefit of others,' Zahir delivered wryly, rolling over to slide a long, hard thigh between hers and nudge her knees apart. 'I want to make love to you...I want to know that you're mine forever.'

Loving the weight of him against her, Saffy gave him

a teasing smile. 'I hope you do appreciate that you will be stuck with me for ever.'

'I was terrified that that might not be the case,' Zahir sliced in, claiming a hungry driving kiss that left her breathless. 'Afraid that you were keeping your options open and planning to ask me for a divorce some day.'

'As long as you can kiss me like that, you're pretty safe,' Saffy teased, watching heat flare in his gaze.

He made love to her with all the scorching passion of his temperament and when she finally subsided in the strong circle of his arms, alight with happiness and the glorious aftermath of incredible physical pleasure, she snuggled close to him. 'I'm not going anywhere away from you ever again,' she swore vehemently.

Zahir grinned, splayed long fingers over her still-flat tummy and gently stroked it. 'So, you'll sleep in a tent with me next time I ask?'

'As long as it has electric and hot and cold running water,' Saffy specified. 'You're really happy about the baby, aren't you?'

A slashing smile scythed across his lean bronzed features. 'Of course I'm excited about the baby, the next generation. We'll be a family as I always dreamt. I still remember the first time I saw you in that store,' he confided huskily. 'And people don't believe in love at first sight.'

'I do...' Lacing her fingers into his thick, tousled black hair, Saffy looked up into his gorgeous eyes with a heart beating like a drum. 'And after what we've been through together and apart, I also believe that a love like that can last for ever…'

'For ever,' Zahir repeated, wrapping both arms round her and pulling her close, knowing that, having lost her once, he would never take the smallest risk of losing her again.

Two years on from that conversation, Saffy soothed her son, Karim, as he fell off his toddler bike for at least the third time and roared with temper and frustration. As soon as his mother set him down again on his sturdy little legs, Karim streaked back to the bike, determined to master the art of riding it so that he could race around the gardens in the company of his female cousins. As she watched her little boy tell the bike off for not doing his bidding, she laughed.

'He doesn't give up easily,' her sister, Kat, commented.

'No, he's like Zahir in that.' Saffy smiled at her sibling, loving the fact that she and Mikhail had come to stay with them in Maraban but aching for the couple at the same time. Kat had recently gone through IVF in Russia in an attempt to conceive but, sadly, the procedure hadn't worked. In another month the couple were set for a second try and Saffy was praying that the treatment would deliver a successful result, for if any woman deserved a child of her own it was Kat, who had raised her three sisters with so much love and support.

'The servants wait on him hand and foot,' Kat commented. 'You'll have to watch that.'

'I do. He tidies up his own toys. Zahir doesn't want him spoiled the same way he was.'

'The way your husband spoils you?' Kat laughed, secure in the knowledge that Saffy was deliriously happy in Maraban.

'Spoiling me gives Zahir a kick,' Saffy confided with a grin, thinking of the vast selection of jewels and luxuries she was continually showered in.

More importantly, Saffy had found a real role to keep her busy in her husband's country. She had participated in making a promotional film of Maraban and had impressed everybody with her skill as a presenter. But then she had thoroughly enjoyed the personalised tour of the various sites of interest with Zahir by her side and had become almost as knowledgeable about his country of birth as he was in the process. The warm welcome of the locals had increased her identification with Maraban as her new home. She had got involved with local charities, now sat on the board of the newest hospital in the city and regularly visited educational institutions. But most precious of all on her terms had been spending an entire week with Zahir and Karim at the orphanage school in South Africa, which she had long supported.

As a rule she usually went to London to see her sisters. Topsy was at university, studying hard and rarely free for more than a weekend, but Emmie often visited London to shop and the twins now got together as often as they could contrive it. Rediscovering her relationship with her sister meant a great deal to Saffy and the process was helped by the reality that both women now had much more in common.

Zahir strode through the door with Mikhail a mere step in his wake. Kat's husband, a Russian billionaire, was currently advising the Marabani government on how best to invest the oil revenues that kept the country afloat. Zahir swept his son off the bike a split second before the child fell again.

'He won't stop trying,' Saffy told her handsome husband. 'He won't give up. He's so like you.'

'But he has your eyes and impatience,' Zahir remarked appreciatively as he set his squirming son down again and watched him head straight back to the demon bike that still wouldn't do what he wanted it to do.

Zahir linked his fingers with Saffy and walked her out onto the terrace. Overhead the sun was sinking in a peach and orange blaze of colour and soon they would sit down to dinner by candlelight and talk long into the night. Just for a moment, even though she was very much enjoying having her sister and her husband as guests, she wished she were alone with Zahir.

He looked down at her with smouldering dark golden eyes and butterflies leapt in her tummy and her mouth ran dry. 'We should get dressed for dinner,' he murmured lazily.

A smile tugging at her lush lips, Saffy leant back against his lean powerful body in an attitude of complete trust, knowing they would end up in bed, loving the fact that he found it as hard to keep his hands off her as she did him. She was deliriously happy in her marriage and Karim's arrival had enriched and deepened the ties between her and Zahir. 'I love you,' she whispered.

'I love you too,' Zahir purred, pressing his mouth hungrily to the base of her throat and making her shiver against him.

* * * * *

SPECIAL EXCERPT FROM

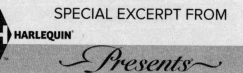

HARLEQUIN

Presents

USA TODAY *bestselling author Lucy Monroe brings you a passionate new duet,* BY HIS ROYAL DECREE, *from Harlequin® Presents®, starting with* ONE NIGHT HEIR *in July 2013.*

* * *

"I will not leave you again." It was a vow, accompanied by the slipping of the ring onto her finger.

Even though it was prompted by her pregnancy and the fact she now carried the heir to the Volyarus throne, the promise in his voice poured over the jagged edges of her heart with soothing warmth. The small weight of the metal band and diamonds on her finger was a source of more comfort than she would ever have believed possible.

She was not sure her heart would ever be whole again, but it did not have to hurt like it had for ten weeks.

"I won't leave you, either."

"I know." A small sound, almost a sigh, escaped his mouth. "Now we must convince your body that it still belongs to me."

"You have a very possessive side."

"This is nothing new."

"Actually, it kind of is." He'd shown indications of a possessive nature when they were dating, but he'd never been so primal about it before. "You're like a caveman."

His smile was predatory, his eyes burning with sensual intent. "You carry my child. It makes me feel *very* possessive, takes me back to the responses of my ancestors."

HPEXP0613-1

Air escaped her lungs in an unexpected whoosh. "Oh."

"I have read that some pregnant women desire sex more often than usual."

"I…" She wasn't sure what she felt in that department right now.

She always seemed to want him and could not imagine her hormones increasing that all too visceral need.

"However, I had not realized the pregnancy could impact the father in the same way." There was no mistaking his meaning.

Maks wanted her. And not in some casual, sex-as-physical-exercise way. The expression in his dark eyes said he wanted to devour her, the mother of his child, sexually.

Gillian shivered in response to that look.

"Cold?" he purred, pushing even closer. "Let me warm you."

"I'm not co—" But she wasn't allowed to finish the thought.

His mouth covered hers in a kiss that demanded full submission and reciprocation.

* * *

Find out what happens when this powerful prince raises the stakes of their marriage of convenience in
ONE NIGHT HEIR, out July 2013!

And don't miss the explosive second story,
PRINCE OF SECRETS, available August 2013.

REQUEST YOUR FREE BOOKS!

2 FREE NOVELS PLUS
2 FREE GIFTS!

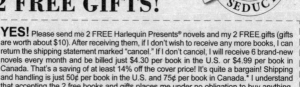

PASSION GUARANTEED SEDUCTION

YES! Please send me 2 FREE Harlequin Presents® novels and my 2 FREE gifts (gifts are worth about $10). After receiving them, if I don't wish to receive any more books, I can return the shipping statement marked "cancel." If I don't cancel, I will receive 6 brand-new novels every month and be billed just $4.30 per book in the U.S. or $4.99 per book in Canada. That's a saving of at least 14% off the cover price! It's quite a bargain! Shipping and handling is just 50¢ per book in the U.S. and 75¢ per book in Canada.* I understand that accepting the 2 free books and gifts places me under no obligation to buy anything. I can always return a shipment and cancel at any time. Even if I never buy another book, the two free books and gifts are mine to keep forever.

106/306 HDN FVRK

Name	(PLEASE PRINT)	
Address		Apt. #
City	State/Prov.	Zip/Postal Code

Signature (if under 18, a parent or guardian must sign)

Mail to the **Harlequin® Reader Service:**
IN U.S.A.: P.O. Box 1867, Buffalo, NY 14240-1867
IN CANADA: P.O. Box 609, Fort Erie, Ontario L2A 5X3

**Are you a current subscriber to Harlequin Presents books
and want to receive the larger-print edition?
Call 1-800-873-8635 or visit www.ReaderService.com.**

* Terms and prices subject to change without notice. Prices do not include applicable taxes. Sales tax applicable in N.Y. Canadian residents will be charged applicable taxes. Offer not valid in Quebec. This offer is limited to one order per household. Not valid for current subscribers to Harlequin Presents books. All orders subject to credit approval. Credit or debit balances in a customer's account(s) may be offset by any other outstanding balance owed by or to the customer. Please allow 4 to 6 weeks for delivery. Offer available while quantities last.

Your Privacy—The Harlequin® Reader Service is committed to protecting your privacy. Our Privacy Policy is available online at www.ReaderService.com or upon request from the Harlequin Reader Service.

We make a portion of our mailing list available to reputable third parties that offer products we believe may interest you. If you prefer that we not exchange your name with third parties, or if you wish to clarify or modify your communication preferences, please visit us at www.ReaderService.com/consumerschoice or write to us at Harlequin Reader Service Preference Service, P.O. Box 9062, Buffalo, NY 14269. Include your complete name and address.

#3153 HIS MOST EXQUISITE CONQUEST

Legendary Finn Brothers

Emma Darcy

...vivacious Lucy Flippence has fallen prey to ...hael Finn, whose reputation is legendary. She might ...only a tick on his to-do list, but even the luxury lifestyle ...n't mask the feelings her secret has forced her to hide....

#3154 A SHADOW OF GUILT

Sicily's Corretti Dynasty

Abby Green

...alentina has always blamed Gio Corretti for her brother's ...eath. But when she needs help, there's only one man she ...an turn to—the cold, inscrutable Gio, whose green eyes ...ash with guilt, regret and a passion that calls to her.

#3155 ONE NIGHT HEIR

By His Royal Decree

Lucy Monroe

Duty comes before desire for Prince Maksim. He knew that when he cut his ties to his mistress Gillian Harris. But when she gets pregnant this fierce royal Cossack must claim his heir and convince her to be his queen!

#3156 HIS BRAND OF PASSION

The Bryants: Powerful & Proud

Kate Hewitt

For billionaire Aaron Bryant, money usually solves everything, but he's not had a problem like this before. One unbridled night of passion with sassy Zoe Parker has left two little lines on a test—turning both their lives upside down.

#3157 THE COUPLE WHO FOOLED THE WORLD
Maisey Yates

Most women would kill to be on Ferro Calvaresi's arm
But Julia Anderson is not most women. When a major
deal requires these two rivals to play nicely...*together*...
the world's hottest new couple beginning to believe th
own lie?

#3158 THE RETURN OF HER PAST
Lindsay Armstrong

Housekeeper's daughter Mia Gardiner knew her feelings
for multimillionaire Carlos O'Connor were foolish. Until s
caught the ruthless playboy's eye. Even now, older and
wiser, Mia has never forgotten the feel of his touch. Ther
like a whirlwind, Carlos returns....

#3159 IN PETRAKIS'S POWER
Maggie Cox

To safeguard her family's future, Natalie makes a deal wit
the devil—Ludo Petrakis. She must travel to Greece—as
his fiancée! But seeing the cracks in Ludo's unshakable
control, she finds that it gets harder to resist the
smoldering tension between them....

#3160 PROOF OF THEIR SIN
One Night with Consequences
Dani Collins

Lauren is pregnant and marriage is the only way to avoid
scandal, but she still bears the scars from the first time she
said "I do." Can she trust the powerful but guarded Paolo
enough to reveal the truth?

You can find more information on upcoming Harlequin®
titles, free excerpts and more at www.Harlequin.com.

HPCNM0613RB